ROGER PULVERS is an author, playwright, theatre director, translator and filmmaker. He has published more than fifty books in Japanese and English, including novels, essays, plays and poetry. Working as assistant to director Oshima Nagisa on *Merry Christmas, Mr. Lawrence* brought him back to Japan and inspired him to become the award-winning playwright, film director and prolific author he is today. His novel, *Hoshizuna Monogatari* (*Star Sand*), which he wrote in Japanese, was published by Kodansha, Japan's largest publisher, in 2015, and subsequently in English and French in 2016 and 2017 respectively. It was released as a film, directed by him, in 2017. His most recent books are the novels, *Half of Each Other* and *Peaceful Circumstances*, his autobiography, *The Unmaking of an American*, and a cultural memoir, *My Japan*, all published by Balestier Press.

ALSO BY ROGER PULVERS

Liv
Half of Each Other
The Honey and the Fires
The Dream of Lafcadio Hearn
Peaceful Circumstances
The Unmaking of an American
My Japan

TRANSLATIONS

Night on the Milky Way Train and Nine Other Stories
by Kenji Miyazawa
The Illusions of Self: Tanka by Takuboku Ishikawa
Wholly Esenin: Poems by Sergei Esenin

THE CHARTER

and thirteen other stories about Japan

ROGER PULVERS

THE CHARTER

and thirteen other stories about Japan

BALESTIER PRESS
LONDON · SINGAPORE

Balestier Press
Centurion House, London TW18 4AX
www.balestier.com

The Charter: And Thirteen Other Stories about Japan
Copyright © Roger Pulvers, 2020

A CIP catalogue record for this book
is available from the British Library.

ISBN 978 1 911221 84 5

Cover illustration by Sophie Pulvers

This book is a work of fiction. The literary perceptions and
insights are based on experience; all names, characters, places,
and incidents either are products of the author's imagination
or are used fictitiously.

CONTENTS

The Charter

I CHARTERED A MEDIUM-SIZED BOAT TO CRUISE ON THE SUMIDA River with members of my immediate family, their closest friends and colleagues from work. It was the 29th of July 2018, the day of my eightieth birthday. This was to be a pleasure cruise, a family get-together with my birthday as the occasion.

My two children and I haven't actually seen much of each other these past few years. We met just once after their mother's funeral. The children are naturally busy with their own lives, and I certainly never expect them to make time for me. Ah, I know that this looks as if I am stoking the dregs of self-pity for all to see. It's nothing of the sort. I am more than content to sit on the sidelines of their lives and watch them slowly pass before me.

We all came together at the Hama Detached Palace at five-thirty in the afternoon. To our good fortune, there was no rain that day. The rainy season had ended; and though the temperature had recorded thirty-two degrees, the heat had dropped off by late afternoon and the air was unseasonably dry. It was as if a cool breeze was skimming off Tokyo Bay, winding its way straight up the river to where we were.

My son's wife Keiko supplied the food for the cruise. After their daughter had graduated university, she started up her own catering business. Keiko is urbane, petite and particularly gorgeous. Though fifty, she is often thought of as being in her late thirties. And having spent two years at a high school in Vancouver, Canada, her English is as impeccable as her manner. These qualities combine to create an extremely successful career catering for the echelons of foreign executives in Tokyo.

No sooner had we boarded the boat than did two tall waitresses —who could have been sisters but for the fact that one was Japanese and the other Korean—appear. Both were dressed entirely in black, bearing tray after tray of exquisite finger food. A tall bearded Italian man in black tie stood behind the bar in the large room with its wrap-around window overlooking the prow. Everyone—there were forty of us altogether—began to eat, drink and plunge into lively conversation with each other before the boat left its mooring.

I sat myself down outside on a wooden bench that skirted the window at the front of the boat. I had taken a large flute of champagne for myself and was more than happy to sit and peer through the glass at everyone. These are the people that Natsuko and I brought into the world, I thought … well, not all of them. But if it hadn't been for our having our son and daughter, then their loved ones and friends would not have come together on this boat on this very day.

I raised my glass, staring across the water as we pulled away from the bank, and whispered to myself, 'Well, Natsuko, we did this, didn't we, you and me? Who would have thought it would be like this when you were twenty-two and I was twenty-five. I miss you, my sweetheart. I miss you so much. You are visible to me on the faces of our children and even on the faces of the people they love.'

I shook my head twice, rapidly, to stave off the tears that were welling in my eyes, and drank nearly half the flute of champagne in two gulps. The boat glided over the water as if not touching it as it left the moat around the palace for the open river. I turned my gaze back into the room. It seemed as if everyone, whether talking or listening, was smiling.

'Hello. What are you doing? Why aren't you inside having fun like everybody else?'

A little girl, dressed in a sleeveless white cotton dress with large red polka dots, was standing behind me by the prow's railing.

'Oh, I didn't see you.'

'That's because you were staring at the water and then at the people in that glass room. I was watching you from when we boarded. I'm very observant, you know.'

'Yes. I can see that.'

'Are you the man who's having the birthday?'

'Yes, I am.'

'Happy birthday.'

'Thank you.'

'How old are you today? No one told me. They just said that some old man was having a birthday.'

'Well, I'm eighty today.'

'Eighty? That's relatively old.'

'Yes, it is. What about you? How old are you?'

She rested both hands on the railing and peered over the water at the opposite bank. She seemed to be contemplating her answer.

'Me? I'm eleven. My name is Nanako.'

'I see. You're very mature for an eleven-year-old.'

'Yes, I know. I think I'm about nineteen in my head. I hope to live to be eighty someday, like you.'

'Oh, I'm sure you will.'

She cocked her head and smirked, as if wondering how I could be so sure of such a thing. I drank the rest of the champagne in the flute and turned to one side, glancing through the curved window at the bar by the far end of the room enclosed by glass.

'I bet you're thinking of having another drink,' said Nanako. 'Well, it is your birthday, after all. Why don't you go inside to be with all the other people?'

'Oh, they're having such a good time as it is. I feel good being out here. I took this very cruise once, a long long time ago. With my wife.'

'I guess if you stay out here, nobody notices you're not there.'

'What?'

She sat down next to me and straightened the hem of her dress over her knees.

'I mean, if you went inside and then came out here, people would wonder what happened to you. It's like being a child. See? Nobody really takes any notice of a little girl. That's why we can take such good photos if we have a mobile phone. Because we're being ignored. We're kind of, you know, invisible. By staying out here, now you're invisible too.'

She unzipped her little white leather shoulder bag and produced a phone, pressing the screen in several places until a photograph of the two waitresses emerging from a small room at the back of the boat appeared.

'See? These two waitresses, who look so much alike, are about to separate and walk on either side of me. But look at their staring eyes. They are holding their trays really high up and looking straight ahead. They don't even see me, though they sense that something, some obstacle or something, is standing in their way. I'm a pillar, or I may as well be one.'

'That's because they're taller than you. They're looking above your head.'

'That's obvious. My phone is about at the level of their belly buttons. And here's the next one I took. It's a man with a pencil moustache.'

'Oh, that's my son, Akihiko. You've definitely captured the squinty look in his eyes.'

'Is he always so glum and serious-looking?'

'Is he? I don't know. I suppose he is. He's a stockbroker. Do you know what a stockbroker is?'

'Not really. Why does he have a pencil moustache? It's not very stylish to have one, you know.'

'Well, I think it's because he admires the writer Tsutsui Yasutaka, who also has one.'

'Is he the man who wrote *The Girl Who Leapt Through Time*, that book?'

'Yes, I think so.'

'Oh. I see. I read it last year. It was all right. No, it was good, I mean. But adults, particularly old men, always seem to think that little girls are so mysterious. I don't like that about old men.'

'Are you mysterious?'

'Me? Or little girls.'

'Well, either.'

'Not at all. We say what we mean, well, some of us do. Maybe that's why adults think we're mysterious, because adults keep most things to themselves. Actually, they're the mysterious ones, if you ask me.'

We both found ourselves staring through the glass into the room. We could see our two reflections side by side in the glass, superimposed on the figures inside. One of the waitresses was now serving sushi on a large rectangular tray that she was holding waist high. Strangely enough, all of the people in the room had their backs to the windows surrounding them.

Nanako sat up. Her torso stretched, as if she had grown taller all of a sudden, and she pointed up river.

'Is that Ryogoku up there?'

'No, we're not there yet. I've told the captain to cruise slowly, to take his time. I want it to feel like time is virtually standing still.'

'Standing still? But we're moving. Look at the water.'

'Yes, I know we are. But if you raise your eyes and look for a moment or two at the sky, you will think you're not. Anyway, you can move through space and feel you are stopped in time.'

'Not what?'

'What?'

'You said, if you look at the sky, you'll think you're not.'

'Not moving.'

We both looked up at the same time. A single elongated cloud the shape of a thin whale, with pale blue streaks running vertically through it, stretched from the horizon behind us all the way to the top of the sky. For a time neither of us said a word.

'I don't think I want to take any more photos now,' said Nanako, replacing her phone in the white bag. 'Are you going to have another drink? I could get you one if you'd rather not go inside.'

'Oh no, thank you. It just makes me think too much of things if I drink.'

'What things?'

'What things? Oh … things.'

'I know,' she said, turning towards me. Her two knees were nearly touching the side of my right knee.

'What do you know?'

'You're sad. Sure, it makes sense. It's your birthday and no one has come out here to talk to you.'

'You have.'

'No, I mean your children, or people. That man with the moustache, your son, has he wished you a happy birthday?'

'Not yet. But he will. They all will.'

'Yeah, sure, when the cake comes out. It's like a Pavolian reaction at birthdays.'

'Pavlovian.'

'Well, it's hard to pronounce, but you know what I mean. I read about it. And is that lady your daughter?'

'Yes, how did you know?'

'She looks like you. What's her name? Is it Mari?'

'Yes, Mari. How do you know that?'

'That man who just got her another glass of white wine. He isn't her husband, is he.'

'You are observant, aren't you!'

'Not in this case. He's my daddy.'

'Oh.'

'He and my mummy are divorced, just like, I guess, your daughter is. I only met her today, though I knew about her existence. My father didn't want me to meet her too early. Now I think they're serious and might get married. If they did, you would be my grandpa.'

'That's a nice thought.'

'Well, it's just the way it would be. Daddy's a budding artist, like your daughter. Well, he's been budding for a long time. They met doing life drawing at some class or something. Personally I don't see how two people can get to like each other when they have to stare for hours on end at a naked man or woman, but that's apparently what happened. He's ten years younger than your daughter, but I don't think that sort of thing matters these days. What matters is whether people are compat … uh, compat …'

'Compatible.'

'Yes, that's what I mean. But where's her daughter? I know she has a daughter.'

'Oh, my granddaughter is in New Zealand.'

'New Zealand? What's she doing there?!'

Nanako seemed to find the very name of the country amusing.

'I'm not sure. Studying or working or just having a good time, or a combination of the three.'

'And those two boys sitting in the corner with their eyeballs stuck to the screens on their phones?'

'My grandsons. They belong to the man with the pencil moustache and his wife, who is now there, see, giving instructions to the two waitresses. Look, see?'

'Sure. I can see her. I still don't like the fact that you are here and they are there.'

Nanako suddenly pointed to the bank ahead on the left side of the boat.

'What's that funny tower?'

'Oh, that's the Reiganjima Water Level Observatory. It calculates the height of the sea. Altitudes around Japan are measured on the basis of those calculations.'

'That is just so cool,' she said, standing to get a better look at the cube-like tower and showing all her teeth in a big smile. 'It's like we're located here right at the centre of Japan now.'

'Is it cool? I'm glad.'

'You don't look glad, though,' she said, sitting back down beside me. 'You definitely look pretty sad. Are you?'

'No. Not at all. It would be nice if my daughter and your daddy got married, wouldn't it be?'

'Are you being ironical? I find it very hard to understand when adults are being ironical.'

'No. I mean it. Why? After all, they seem to have so much in common.'

'Is that why people get married? Because they have things in common? Like drawing naked people?'

'Some people do it like that, because they look at the world in the same way.'

'I don't want to go inside. I want to stay out here with you.'

'Thank you. But we will be going inside when we get to Ryogoku. That's when the cake will be brought out.'

'Oh. Then you will be officially eighty, I guess, when you blow out the candles.'

'I suppose so.'

'You get a year older the instant the fire of the candles goes out, you know. I find it funny, though, that people actually celebrate getting older. You know, I find it morbid.'

'You do?'

'Yes. Why celebrate it? Did you see that pine tree in the palace garden before we left?'

'The ancient one? The one that's three hundred years old?'

'Yes, that one. That's really old, even for somebody as old as you, isn't it?'

'Yes, it certainly is,' I chuckled.

'It's 3.75 times older than you.'

'What?'

'That pine tree. You're eighty, right? And the tree is, let's say, exactly three hundred. Three hundred divided by eighty is 3.75. That means that the tree has seen almost four people like you come and go in its lifetime. I can do calculations like that in my head. But, okay, I do use the calculator on my phone when sums go over ten thousand.'

The single long streaky cloud seemed to have flattened out over the entire sky. It was as if a gauze-like white cover was stretched from one horizon to the other, with the sun a faint ball behind it. The water's surface had lost all reflection. The bridges over the Sumida River were casting no shadow. The boat seemed to be stopped dead in the middle of the river. As I looked into the glass-enclosed room, all the people there seemed to have ceased to move or talk with each other.

Nanako and I sat for some time without speaking.

'Is that the Ryogoku Bridge?' she finally said, pointing ahead.

'Yes, that's it,' I said, lifting myself up, carefully standing my champagne flute on the bench and stepping up to the railing.

Nanako stood beside me. We both looked in the direction of the bridge.

'The original bridge was built about three hundred and fifty years ago,' I said. 'It was like an arc … like …'

'A rainbow made out of wood?'

'Well, when the sky is full of colour above it, it would be, yes, I suppose. The old bridge arced upwards towards the middle then down again, not like straight bridges today.'

She squinted intently at the modern steel bridge in the distance, smiling and nodding, as if she could imagine what the old bridge that had not existed for ages had looked like.

'There's a woodblock print of fireworks bursting into the sky over the old bridge by Hiroshige. It …'

Nanako shook her head over and over, giggling, at first under her breath and then in loud squeaks.

'Is that funny?'

'No, it's just that name you just said.'

'Hiroshige?'

Now she was laughing uncontrollably, with little tears streaming down her cheeks.

'That's such a funny name,' she finally said, gasping for breath. 'I've never heard that name before.'

Despite the gifted observations about others and her clever calculations, she was, after all, only eleven years old. I picked up my flute, tipping its only drop into my mouth, placed it on its side in the crack between the two planks of the bench and sat down.

The people in the room were once again engaged in buoyant conversation with each other. The waitresses with the food trays were nowhere to be seen, but the bartender, surrounded by friends and colleagues of my children, was busier than before, opening bottles of beer and pouring one glass of wine after another.

'If you're going to be my grandfather, can I sit on your lap?' said Nanako, folding her arms over her chest and pursing her lips.

'That would be very nice, Nanako-san,' I said.

She sat on my lap as the boat moved gradually over the water towards Ryogoku Bridge.

'You know, Nanako-san, the great fireworks display is on this evening. I've timed our arrival for seven o'clock, which is five minutes before the first firework lights up the sky. The cake will be brought out, the candles will be lit, everyone will sing "Happy Birthday" to me and I will blow out the candles precisely at five minutes after seven. The light from the candles will go out. But that light will really fly up and away, lighting up the sky … my own little sparks. Have you ever seen the fireworks over the Ryogoku Bridge?'

'No,' she said, putting her hands on my knees. 'I can't say that I have.'

'They're beautiful. Very beautiful. They are *wabi*. Do you know what that means?'

'No.'

'*Wa* is "Japanese", and *bi* is "fire". It's the ancient word for a certain type of firework. You see, Nanako-san, the colours in the sky here above you and me will be varied, from red and green and purple and lots of other colours, including silver and gold. Their fire is like ancient coins sent up high into the sky and then smashed to bits.'

'What colour is wabi?'

'Wabi? Wabi is black.'

'Black? But my art teacher said that black isn't really a colour.'

'That's right. But the fire that is wabi is a very special black that can be seen against the sky. It is something that is both visible and invisible at the same time. Did you know there was a light like that?'

'You're funny, Grandpa.'

'Am I?'

'Yes. I like you. Will you promise to be my grandpa?'

'Yes.'

'Say "Yes, I promise you, Nanako-san". Say that.'

'I promise you, Nanako-san.'

She beamed a magnificent smile at me. It was the same smile I saw on her face when she pointed to the tower and said we were at the centre of Japan.

After that we both went inside, holding hands. At seven the cake was brought out. Everyone sang. At five minutes after seven I blew out the candles, in a single blow, if I say so myself. Well, it was only eight candles, one to mark each decade of my life.

And at the very instant that the candle flames went out, a hair's-breadth thread of fire shot up into the sky, arcing down and vanishing before it could strike the ground on the opposite bank of the river. A huge flower of light burst into the sky out of nowhere, Nanako squeezed my hand tightly and looked up to me … and I felt the happiest I have been since my dear and beautiful wife Natsuko passed away. The blackness of the sky over Ryogoku that night was so bright that it could be seen farther than the eye could see … Natsuko, Natsuko, I touched your face in my reflection on the curved glass of the boat, I felt your warmth in the flames of my little coloured candles, I saw you—it is you—inside the radiant black light of the sky … you.

We all left the boat at Ryogoku and went our separate ways. But before we parted, Nanako made me promise that I would be her grandpa 'even,' she said, 'if my daddy and your daughter don't get married to each other in the end.'

That sort of thing didn't seem to matter to Nanako … nor did it matter to me.

Daisuke's Graduation

THE FIRST TWO EMAILS THAT I SENT TO MY EX-WIFE WENT unanswered. This came as no surprise to me. I had become used to the silent treatment from her since the year after we returned from our honeymoon in Hawaii twelve years ago. But this time I was not about to put up with being ignored.

After waiting three days I wrote the following to her:

Eiko. Frankly, aren't you sick and tired of this particular pattern of communication that we have fallen into, either by chance or design? I sent you two emails the other day and you do not even grant me the courtesy of a reply. I will not plead with you (as I once did), and I will not lose my temper (as I often did in the past). PLEASE let us stop this and at least be civil to each other.

I am writing to you because I am moving back to Tokyo and want to see Daisuke. I have a right to see my own son and attend his graduation from primary school. It is important to him that his father be present at the ceremony. Please consider his future. He will want to have this as a memory when he is my age.

We need not sit side by side in the school hall. If you wish, I will stand silently in the back against the wall as my son passes in the procession. I won't acknowledge your presence. But I want to be there!

Tatsuhiko

After several minutes of hesitation I pressed the return button, sending the mail to her. It was 10pm New York time. I poured myself a single malt whisky, dropped two small cubes of ice into the glass and sat down to watch an old western, starring John Wayne, on cable television. After twenty minutes I stood up, walked to my computer and opened my email file. I was, I admit, shocked to see that Eiko had replied. This is what she wrote:

If we have fallen into a pattern of communication, as you say, who is to blame? You talk about rights as a father, but I would just like to ask you about the other 'rights' which you seem to ignore so conveniently. Does a father have the right to default on alimony payments? Does a father have the right to cheat on his wife with another woman … or should I say 'women' … less than a year after the wedding? Does a father who never went to a single sports day at his son's school, never once attended a class on parents' day, never once took the slightest interest in his son's development … does such a father have any 'rights' left to him at all?

You are, of course, free to come back to Tokyo for a visit or to live or whatever. But you are NOT to come to Daisuke's graduation ceremony. I have already told him and Shimoda-sensei (that's the name of his sixth-grade teacher, for your information) that 'Daddy' is too busy with work in New York to attend.

That was how the email ended. No name. Just coldly, 'too busy … to attend.'

I immediately typed a reply. It was a rare occurrence to get any message from Eiko. I knew that if I hesitated now I would probably not hear from her again.

Eiko. I am grateful for your message. I won't try to justify things I did in the past, okay? Shortly before we finally separated six years ago, I'm sure you will remember the arguments that dragged long into nights. After I was transferred to New York, it was always I who phoned you and paid for the calls. I ask you now, Why should

Daisuke continue to suffer over our incompatibility? And as for the matter of women, the whole thing was not as important to me as you have always made it out to be. There were only two, as I have told you over and over again. Well, maybe three, counting that Canadian exchange student at Showa Women's University, but she was using me, when you come down to it. You should at least give me credit for telling you everything.

I stopped typing. No, this was definitely not the sort of thing to write to an ex-wife. In addition, I couldn't definitely remember if I had told her about the Canadian exchange student or not. It would only add fuel to a smouldering fire. I highlighted the text from 'And as for the matter of women' to 'telling you everything', took a sip of the now watery whisky and pressed 'Delete'. The shooting of guns coming from the television set suddenly became inordinately loud. I took the remote control device from my shirt pocket, turned the set off and continued my message to Eiko.

Okay, I accept responsibility for all my past actions, bad and indifferent. I'm not proud of everything. But believe me, I didn't do anything to hurt you or Daisuke. These things happen in life. A man doesn't plan everything, you know.

Can't we erase what is past and go on from here? I am asking you now, Eiko, if we can do that. I do not expect you to see me or talk to me when I'm back in Tokyo. All I want is to see our son walk down the aisle among his friends. I won't even smile at him, if that's what you wish. I'll just nod once, so he knows it's really me. All I want is to be in the same room with him on the day of his graduation.

From Tatsuhiko

Without hesitation I clicked the return button. I felt a deep sense of relief, the kind that I felt as a child when I wrote down all the bad things that had happened to me in a notebook, then rubbed them out with a rubber until there was no trace left. I was sure that Eiko would see reason. I quickly poured myself another whisky, now adding no ice. I sat back in my leather armchair and once again turned on the television. The shooting had come to an end, and four men were seated at a round table in a saloon, playing cards in silence. John Wayne was nowhere to be seen.

It was nearly midnight when the movie ended and I returned to my computer. I clicked on 'Send/Receive'. There was one new email, which seemed to take an age before downloading. It was from Eiko. I opened it. There were two sentences on a single line, without greeting at the beginning or name at the end. It simply said:

Please yourself. You always have.

I AWOKE AFTER EIGHT THE NEXT DAY, A MONDAY. I HAD TOLD MY secretary that I wouldn't be coming into the office that day. I had already cleaned out my desk and said my goodbyes to the staff. I needed one day to myself before going home to Tokyo.

I decided to have breakfast near my apartment at Macchiato Espresso Bar on East 44th St. But before leaving my apartment I turned on my computer and opened my mail, out of habit more than anything else. I didn't expect to see the message from my ex-wife, sent at 4:20pm Japan time.

Tatsuhiko-san. When I wrote 'please yourself' I did not mean for you to think of it as an insult. I'm sorry. I didn't mean to say that to you. At first I really didn't want you to come to Daisuke's graduation. I even once told Daisuke that he was like his friend Haruna. Haruna's daddy is dead.

But I realise that you are his father and you were once my husband, too. You remember where the school is? It's at Chitose Funabashi. Please call us when you arrive in Tokyo. But please call in the afternoon between 4 o'clock and 5:30, no earlier or later.

Your ex-wife and Daisuke's mummy, Eiko

I rubbed my eyes and reread the message. I could not believe that Eiko could suddenly be so tender and understanding. I immediately typed out a reply to her, sent it, hopped over my two suitcases in the living room as if they were hurdles on a race track, left my apartment, locked the three locks on the door and walked briskly down the stairs, taking two steps at a time. Gordon, the doorman, who sported a trim handlebar moustache, opened the building's front door for me.

'Good morning, Mr T,' he said, with an easy bow.

'Good morning, Gordon.'

'We're gonna miss you around here, Mr T. Except for one thing that I'm not gonna miss.'

'Oh?'

'Yes, sir. I'm glad you're not gonna be livin' here now 'cause of your name. Jumpin' Jesus, Mr T, I swear, you got the hardest dang name to pronounce ever since that Mr Kryzolewski, or somethin', I dunno, lived here, and I'm goin' back forty-five years now. Darned if I know how you pronounce it yourself!'

'I'm sorry,' I said, being utterly Japanese in apologising for something that caused another person inconvenience, whatever its nature.

'Oh, heck, don't be sorry, Mr T. That's your name and you mustn't apologise for it. It's all you got.'

I shook hands with Gordon and ran diagonally across Lexington Ave., dodging a taxi. I had one thought only in my mind: The sight of his father standing against the back wall would be etched in Daisuke's memory after all. No one could prevent me now from attending his graduation.

This is what I had written to Eiko:

Eiko. Thank you for being so gracious. I owe you an apology for many many things, but perhaps this is not the time or way to make it. I will telephone you at the time you specified in your email when I get back to Tokyo. I am staying with my mother at Kyodo, so it's not far from Daisuke's school.

Talk soon

Tatsu

The morning was unusually warm for early March in New York. I walked up Lexington Ave. until reaching 44th St. and turned right, suddenly realising that I had been whistling what was known in America as the Sukiyaki Song, 'Look Upward as you Walk'. I stopped whistling and stood on the corner for a moment, gazing far down, then up, Lexington Ave. Hundreds of people were marching, at a brisk pace, uptown and down, heading for the gates of the subway. Why, I wondered, did I have to call Eiko in the late afternoon? Perhaps she had a new job that started early in the morning. No matter. What mattered was that I was on my way back to Tokyo, where I would see my only child, my son, Daisuke.

I phoned Eiko on Thursday afternoon precisely at 4:30. It was strange being in my parents' home, where Eiko and I had lived for a year after returning from our honeymoon. We hadn't known then that Eiko was already three months pregnant with our daughter, Tomiko. When Tomiko died in her cot, age three months … just stopped breathing … just didn't wake up … I thought that Eiko would never recover from the trauma. But she was already pregnant then with Daisuke, and perhaps it was Daisuke's birth that allowed her to return to her former self.

'Hello,' said the voice at the other end of the line.
'Hello, Eiko-san? It's me, Tatsuhiko.'
'This is Daisuke.'
'Oh, Daisuke. It's daddy. You sound just like your mother.'

There was a silence. I continued.

'Daddy's come back. I mean, I'm coming to live here now. Isn't that good?'

'Uh-huh.'

'I'm coming to see you at your graduation next week. Isn't that good?'

'Uh-huh.'

'Oh, Daisuke, it's so good to talk with you.'

There was another silence, then Daisuke spoke.

'It's good to talk with you, too, Daddy.'

I must confess, tears welled in my eyes when I heard Daisuke say, 'daddy'. I was now more determined than ever to see him as soon as I could, even before his graduation ceremony.

'Do you think I could see you sometime, I mean, pretty soon?'

'I dunno.'

'No, I mean, not at home or school. Like, somewhere else. Do you think you could come to grandma's here at Kyodo?'

'If mummy would let me I could.'

'Oh, she'll let you … no, perhaps she wouldn't.'

'Daddy?'

'Yes.'

'Do you think you and mummy could meet together, just once? I could come too. Then you could see me and you could see mummy, too.'

'I don't think she would like that.'

Then he said something that struck me as slightly strange.

'Didn't you read the email from mummy? She said so. She said she was sorry, didn't she?'

'Do you read her emails?'

'No, I don't, but.'

'Well,' I said, 'whatever. So, tell your mother that I phoned and that I'm at grandma's, okay?'

'I'll tell her.'

'Good. Bye.'

'Bye, Daddy.'

I held the receiver to my ear for some seconds. Daisuke had not yet clicked off.

'Daisuke? … Daisuke?'

'Yes, Daddy.'

'Well, bye.'

'Bye.'

Now he hung up. I listened to the buzz coming through my receiver, as if it held some additional message for me about the feelings of my son and my ex-wife.

It wasn't until Friday afternoon, a few minutes after four, that I had a call from the house at Soshigaya Okura in which Daisuke and Eiko were still living. I had spent the last twenty-four hours almost entirely in bed, not wishing to go out or see anybody. My mother handed me the landline's cordless receiver.

'It's for you,' she said, shuffling out of the bedroom I had slept in as a child.

'Hello?'

'May I please speak with Mr Tatsuhiko Takebayashi?'

'Speaking. Who is calling, please?'

'This is Daisuke Takebayashi.'

'Daisuke! It's daddy! I didn't recognise your voice again. You sound so adult. Is your mother home now?'

'No, she's … um, no, but, she's out right just now.'

'Oh. Did you tell her that I phoned yesterday?'

'Well, daddy, I …um, I sort of did….'

'So, what did she say?'

'She said she wanted, I mean, to meet with you, together with me, so it's okay, to discuss my graduation and stuff.'

'Is that what she said?'

'Yep. Really, what she said. She told me to thank you for the emails and that you should go tomorrow morning, Saturday, at 10am, to Alpes coffee shop in Seijo Gakuenmae. She said that you know where it is because, I mean, I don't know how to get there but she said you and me and she had coffee there sometimes, but I don't remember because I was too little and I didn't even drink coffee then or even now.'

'Yes, I remember. Okay. But you'll be there too, won't you? Daddy really wants to see you.'

'I'll be there, Daddy. Sure. Okay, bye. See you tomorrow. Gotta go now. Bye, Daddy.'

Daisuke hung up. I couldn't imagine what it was that had softened Eiko's attitude towards me. We had met when we were both students of English at Keio University. In fact, she was always better at the language than I was, and it was she who aspired to life abroad, not me. It's a shame that by the time I was posted to New York we were already separated.

I woke up on Saturday morning feeling a new man. It was as if I had spent the past four days, in the air and in Tokyo, in a trance, with each hour disconnected from the one before it. I would have to go to the office at Otemachi on Monday, but for now I had two days to myself ... and for my family.

I decided to walk from Kyodo to Seijo, leaving the house just before nine. The branches of the trees along Shiroyama Ave. had sprouted small light-green leaves. Far in the distance I could see Mt Fuji, still covered in snow. I crossed the Odakyu Line tracks and turned up the narrow shopping street at Soshigaya Okura station. The same shops that had been there twelve years ago were there ... the stationery store, the tea shop with its roasting machine in front sending out a cloud of bitter smoke ... '*Maido maido* (Thanks for your patronage),' said the short stocky bald vegetable man. 'What'll it be today?'

I stopped in my tracks. I had not bought vegetables from this man for more than nine years, and here he was greeting me as if I was still passing before his shop every day and making purchases.

'Well, Mr Takebayashi, so nice to see you,' said an elderly woman, gently tapping my elbow.

I swivelled about and stared at her. She looked familiar, but I could not place her.

'It's Morita. I'm Morita, don't you remember? Your wife taught my granddaughter English and we used to live across the street from you then. We moved, but I believe your wife is still there, isn't she?'

'Oh, yes. I remember. Mrs Morita. You used to put the Soka Gakkai newspaper in our mailbox.'

'Yes, that's me! Still do,' she giggled, 'even though I don't live near you anymore. Your boy must be very grown up by now. What was his name? I can't remember names anymore.'

'Daisuke.'

'Yes, that's it, Daisuke. My granddaughter's now studying English at ICU, thanks to your wife's guidance. She's such a marvellous teacher, your wife. Even I picked up a few phrases just by sitting nearby.'

She chuckled to herself, bowed and said …

'Well, goodbye. You have done so much for my family, Mr Takebayashi.'

She walked a few steps up the street, bowed to the vegetable man and disappeared into the dry cleaner's.

It was 9:50 when I arrived at Seijo Gakuenmae station. I walked up to the Mitsubishi Bank building, now Mitsubishi Tokyo UFJ, passed the old Sasaya wine shop, which was still there, and back down to Alpes. I stepped into the coffee shop at 9:58. Several well-dressed ladies were lined up at the counter buying cakes. Straight ahead, towards the back, I caught sight of Daisuke. He looked the same to me until he stood up and waved. Then I saw that he was a head taller than when I had last seen him. He sat back down. I walked towards the table, which was surrounded on three sides by mirrors. I could see the left hand and left knee of someone else behind the wall that jutted out.

For a moment I felt dizzy. I grasped the bannister that went up to the second floor and took several deep breaths. The clock was playing its little trick on me again, now disjointing not hours but minutes, forcing them together even when their jagged edges didn't fit with each other. The words that I had rubbed out of my childhood notebook had once become invisible, but now they were reappearing in my mind's eye, one after another, coming back to me with the vengeance of time.

I sat opposite Eiko. Daisuke was between us, his back to one of the mirrored walls. For some time we said nothing to each other. Daisuke was all smiles.

'Well,' he finally said, 'aren't you at least going to say hello to each other? Okay, then, I will. Hello, Daddy. This is mummy. Hello, Mummy, this is daddy. Mummy, Daddy, very nice to meet you.'

Eiko sat with her head bowed, fingering her little rolled towel. She lifted the glass of ice water with its sliced lemon in it, but put it back down without drinking. A young waitress came to our table and placed a rolled towel and a glass of water in front of me.

'Do you wish to order?' she asked.

'Yes, thank you,' said Daisuke. 'We will have one hot coffee, one Royal Milk Tea and, um, I'll have freshly squeezed orange juice, please. I know it's expensive, but this is a special occasion.'

The waitress glanced at me, then at Eiko, as if to get approval for the order. I nodded to her, and she turned and walked away.

'Well, so what is this all about?' said Eiko.

'All about?' I asked. 'Nothing. Why? I thought we might discuss Daisuke's graduation. Oh, by the way, I just met Mrs Morita, you know, the one whose granddaughter you tutored. She's at International Christian University.'

Eiko said nothing. Again she lifted her glass, this time taking a long drink. I could see that her hand was slightly trembling as she held the glass against her lips.

'We can discuss my graduation later,' said Daisuke. 'Right now, I've got a really good idea. I really don't want that orange juice. It's too expensive, anyway. So, I'll cancel my order, 'cause I'd rather go to the great manga shop at the station and then you two could discuss my graduation here just by yourselves. Isn't that a good idea?'

Daisuke stood up.

'Just a minute,' I said. 'Sit down.'

'Don't order Daisuke around like that,' said Eiko. 'You come home for the first time in years and already you're ordering him around.'

'It's okay, Mummy. I don't mind being ordered around by daddy. Okay, I'll have my orange juice, but only on one condition. You and daddy have to have a conversation. If you don't want me to understand it, you can speak English. I don't understand English yet.'

'You're determined to go to this graduation, are you?' she said.

'Yes, I am. You said in your email that, after all, I am Daisuke's father and that I could come to the school at Chitose Funabashi.'

'I didn't write anything of the sort.'

'Look,' said Daisuke, picking up his rolled towel and twisting it. 'You've only been here a few minutes and already you start fighting again. Who cares about some stupid email? The important thing is that I'll have both my parents at my graduation. Think of poor Haruna-chan. She only has a mummy. Isn't that awful?'

'Why did you ask me to phone you in the late afternoon?' I asked.

'Me? I didn't. I'm out every weekday in the late afternoon, teaching English to a group of retired executives at Machida. They pay more than three times what I get from other groups.'

I stared at Daisuke, who was no longer smiling. A young man arrived at our table with a tray of drinks.

'Fresh orange juice?'

'That's me,' said Daisuke. 'And the Royal Milk Tea is for her and the coffee is for him.'

It was strange to hear Daisuke call Eiko and me 'her' and 'him'.

The waiter put the drinks on the table and left.

'I will never understand why someone takes an order and then someone else brings it,' I said, shaking my head.

'Why? Don't they do that in *New York*?'

Her irony when she said 'New York' was all too obvious.

There was a long pause, broken by Daisuke.

'Gee, this juice is delicious. But I guess it should be, considering the price.'

'So, where are you staying?' she asked me.

'I told you in my email. With my mother. At Kyodo.'

'I didn't know that.'

'Dad, would you like some sugar in your coffee? It looks awfully strong like that. Or maybe some milk?'

Suddenly, both Eiko and I found ourselves staring at Daisuke, who was making an extraordinarily loud noise drinking the last drops of orange juice through a straw.

'Daisuke?'

'Yes, Daddy.'

'Have you been home in the afternoons, say, roughly between four and five?'

'I think so.'

'And do you use your mother's email?'

'Yes, he does,' said Eiko. 'It was Daisuke who set up the new computer when he was only nine.'

Why had it taken me so long to realise? Daisuke had written Eiko's emails, instructing me to call when she was out, so that he could arrange a meeting between the two of us. It was his only way of getting his parents to meet each other.

Now followed the longest silence of all.

Eiko and I found ourselves looking at each other for the first time. It was strange to look into her face. She had changed little since the first years of our marriage. Her skin was still smooth and radiant.

I stared at my face in the mirror beside Eiko's head. My face didn't look like my own! Was time playing the final trick on me, as if telling me, 'You are not the same man as you were in the past, Tatsuhiko. From now on you risk losing sight of yourself!'

Better not look, I told myself. Better to avoid your own gaze in the future. I looked at Eiko's long brown hair, falling over her shoulders, then away from her hair and myself. Eiko was looking in the mirror that was behind me, fixing her gaze on something in it. Did she recognise herself as the woman who once married the man in front of her?

Out of the blue Daisuke shouted, and all of the people in Alpes turned towards the three of us in a frozen stare. Daisuke's shouting was innocent and full of glee. I remember that kind of voice. I had it when I was a boy his age.

'Daddy, look,' he cried. 'Mummy, look. The mirrors. See? You can see yourselves and me reflected in these mirrors. So that means that really there are not just three of us, but six of us. See? We're sitting together now, all six of us. We are like we are now, but we're still like we were a long time ago when mummy and daddy lived together, with me. Mummy, daddy and Daisuke in the mirror … that's us as we were. I see it. We're like then and now at the very same time. Look and you'll see. Just … look!'

I stared into the mirror that was behind Eiko, and she stared into the mirror behind me. But I could only see myself as I am today. What Eiko saw in the mirror, I cannot imagine.

The three of us sat there, surrounded by mirrors, for what seemed an age.

No one was saying a word, not even Daisuke.

A Kind of Elegance

An announcement, a single sentence in length, appeared in the lower right corner of the front page of *The Kokoro*, the English-language monthly published by the Miyamoto School of Tea in Kyoto.

Ms Barbara Zimmermann, formerly interpreter for Iemoto and instructor of beginner-level pupils of the tea ceremony in the school's Daidai-Kai, has returned permanently to her home in Hamburg, Germany.

Not one pupil at the Miyamoto School of Tea could fathom why Barbara, of all people, should leave Japan, let alone 'permanently'.

'She was a kind of ambassador of tea,' said Lonnie Kipsky, by far the leading American expert on the yarn used at the base of the bamboo bristles on a tea whisk. Kipsky, the first nonJapanese to reveal the reason why the colour of this yarn varied from black to white to red, depending on the school of tea using it, co-owned with Paddy McNeil an Irish-style pub on Kitayama Blvd. called 'The Hawk's Well'.

'No person was closer to Iemoto than Barbara,' said Kipsky. 'An Iemoto, or the head of the school, is like an emperor, and Barbara was the emperor's first lady.'

The only person who could explain Barbara's sudden return to her homeland was her Australian flat mate, Bunny.

'Barb and I shared this traditional Japanese house up in Matsugasaki. Made me feel just at home with its dunny out the back. The house had been in Iemoto's family for yonks, or rather, it seems, not directly in his family but in his wife's. Even his best tea ceremony utensils an' bowls an' stuff came from her. After the war the Miyamoto family, despite their prestige from being an established house of the tea ceremony, was, like, livin' off the smell of an oily rag, and so his wife's father, who apparently came back from China with heaps of gold he "acquired", in inverted commas, from the Chinese, bought up all the most valuable tea bowls an' stuff from old Kyoto families and gave them to Iemoto along with his daughter. Some say Iemoto married his wife for her bowls.

'It was a bargain, any way you look at it, and it gave Iemoto the tools of his trade and his wife's family respectability, not to mention protection from investigation into the old man's wartime "China connection". The tea ceremony is, like, a sacred cow in Japan. It's got to be above approach, which means that any scandals have to be kept hush-hush … and nobody does hush-hush better than a Japanese.'

What Bunny meant was 'above reproach', but she was right about the swift rise in social status of the Miyamoto family, not to mention the bulging bank balance of the Miyamoto School of Tea in Kyoto, controlled entirely by the Iemoto himself.

Barbara had come to the Miyamoto School thanks to the introduction of her grandfather, Heinrich Zimmermann, who had been a prisoner of war of the Soviets in Siberia. He met the present-day Iemoto at a POW camp in the mountains west of Lake Baikal, where the prisoners were forced to mine uranium to be used in Soviet atomic weapons. Both men were made to work fourteen hours a day in uranium mines. Iemoto was allowed to return to Japan in 1948. Zimmermann, however, did not reach his hometown of Hamburg until 1954. He soon went into the business of importing coffee from Addis Ababa, working out of the Coffee Exchange located on an island on the Elbe River in Hamburg.

On a business trip to Japan in the early 1970s Zimmermann had a reunion with his old *Genosse* (comrade) Lt Miyamoto, thinking it ironical that both of them had become rich and powerful trading on what he called 'stimulating beverages'. Until his dying day at the age of ninety-two in 2012 Heinrich Zimmermann was unable to understand how his comrade from the POW camp in Siberia had become so rich 'just for whisking around tea powder in an old chipped bowl', and Barbara had been unable to explain it to him to his satisfaction. All she could say was, 'One of those chipped bowls you mention can cost tens of thousands of euros. How much is a coffee cup?'

Barbara had dropped out of her painting course at the Hamburg University of Art after only a year's study because, in her own words, 'There were a few beautiful things there and a few new things as well, but unfortunately I found the beautiful things not new and the new things not beautiful.' Her grandfather, who had always had an anti-authoritarian streak in his personality, urged her to go to Kyoto 'where my old comrade from the POW camp in Siberia owns some sort of culture school.'

And so Barbara found herself enrolled as a beginner at the Miyamoto School of Tea in Japan's ancient capital.

At first Iemoto treated her as he did all his other pupils, whether Japanese or nonJapanese, that is, with a nonchalant disdain. Barbara was despatched to the Daidai-Kai, which was the name given to the group of some twenty nonJapanese, mostly Americans, studying the tea ceremony. '*Daidai-Kai* means "bitter orange group" in English,' explained Iemoto to Abby Eisenglass, who had gone down to Kyoto to interview him for an article in The Japan Times.

'The sound can also mean "many generations' group". We Japanese,' explained Iemoto to her, 'we like things that have more than one meaning, unlike you foreigners whose expressions are limited to one meaning only.'

'Iemoto is so, I mean, aloof,' said Barbara one night to Bunny, as the two of them prowled the bars of Kiyamachi in downtown Kyoto looking for one with a happy hour.

'Yeah,' said Bunny. 'Hey, look at those two awesome blokes standing by the alleyway going into Pontocho. Maybe they know where we can find a good happy hour.'

'Bunny! We were talking about Iemoto.'

'Oh yeah. So, yeah, y'know, he acts, like, kinda aloof, but he really keeps an eye on the foreigners, especially the foreign girls. You yourself know he has, like, a marriage of convenience. He married his wife for her equipment. Oh, that didn't sound very kosher. I mean, tea equipment.'

As Bunny looked back on those early days of Barbara's stay in Kyoto, she began to notice a change taking place in her flat mate.

'At first Barb was really a live wire, like, outgoing, full of life. And she was clever, like, really really clever. She got the hang of tea quicker than any of us, even quicker than Lonnie, who was, like, totally amazing. Lonnie was the only foreigner that Iemoto really trusted. He let him into his inner circle, which was all made up of stuck-up Japanese types, y'know, the kind who think the light shines outta his bum and want to bathe in its reflection. Anyway, so Iemoto knew that Lonnie had dealings with some, like, shady people in Osaka who would go down to Okinawa to get coke and ice from American soldiers stationed down there, an' Lonnie knew too that if he ever got caught Iemoto could protect him because Iemoto had these really good connections with the police in Kyoto, so if for any reason Lonnie had to leave Japan quick-smart, Iemoto could get him on a plane out of Kansai that day.

'Anyway, so it wasn't long before Barb asked me if Iemoto had ever tried to score on one of the foreign girls in the Daidai-Kai, an' I said that no one sort of talked about that, but that there was this Hawaiian yonsei named Cindy who, they say, and I'm not sayin' it myself only that *they* say that, so, that she had to have an abortion and then that she was flown back to Honolulu right after it, but no one was ever able to prove that it was Iemoto's.

'But I did tell Barb that I wouldn't mind rubbing myself over his tummy once, I mean, I know he's a lot older, no one knows his exact age, but he's got to be in his eighties, but apparently he hasn't lost … um, lost his, um, y'know, like, mojo.

'I was really shocked by Barb's reaction. "Not me. No tummy rubbing for me, Bunny. I came here to find true art … and I am finding it in the silence and tranquility and harmonious beauty of the tea ceremony. I came to Kyoto to find myself, not someone else. I don't need outer stimulation".

'Yeah, it all started with that "harmonious beauty" thingo, but it developed really fast after that. Now, let me make one thing really clear, okay? Barb did not leave Japan because of her affair with Iemoto, that's for sure. No way. He was always correct with her in public in a fatherly—or should I say, grandfatherly—way. And she didn't mind either that he had lots of women, especially after Viagra was legalised in Japan, which sort of made it, like, possible in the first place. Actually, before then Lonnie was getting it for him from America, I mean the Viagra. Anyway, so long as his other women were Japanese, Barbara didn't mind. After all, Iemoto was a famous man in Japan and Japanese women, especially women doing the tea ceremony in small towns around the country, worshipped him. It was said that he once held a tea ceremony with six young women in an ancient teahouse entirely in the nude. It was before the era of mobile phones so there are no photos, like, sent around the world, but someone in one of those trashy Japanese weekly magazines apparently found out about it and wrote an article titled *Chashitsu de no Hadaka no Tsukiai*, which Lonnie kinda loosely translated as "The Naked Truth Revealed in a Teahouse".

'Barb laughed it all off. She said Iemoto was taking the message of the beauty and harmony of tea to the provinces and that when he went overseas, like, he was given all these awards by governments and monarchs an' things, but that he was above all the cares of other people and just wanted to plant the seeds of Japanese culture everywhere, and so I said something like, yeah, seeds is right, but I think that kinda when over her head, because Barb was really sweet and naive-like, but, anyway, it was clear as day that Barb was in love with him by then anyway. Here he was old enough to be her grandfather an' she adored him, search me why. I think it might have been because he kinda worshipped her too in his own way. Maybe he has a thing for the Germans, who knows.

'It was all okay, I mean, we just went on like that until everything went pear-shaped. Barb became, I mean, disillusioned. Yeah, that's the word. She lost all her illusions about Iemoto and the tea ceremony and Kyoto and beauty and harmony that were really all just built up, y'know, in her mind anyway.

'It was a really stifling mid-August night, the kind where the sweat just drips off you like rain. The air in Kyoto was so still, like oxygen had been drained out of it leaving you nothing to breathe with. The man who had taken over Barb's grandpa's business had come to Kyoto, and Iemoto was kinda throwing a dinner for him at this fancy Gion restaurant called "Chez Igarashi", where the owner-chef, whose name was Igarashi, boasted that Paul Bocuse had once dropped down onto his hands and knees in front of him and called him "the new grandmaster of root vegetable cuisine". Anyway, apparently the portions there are so small you needed an electron microscope to see what you're eating.

'Barb told me about the dinner because she was called there to interpret for Iemoto since she spoke German and Japanese. Iemoto was pointing out the name of the eel they were served, *yatsume-unagi.* He said that it had eight dots on its side and that's why it was called "eight-eye eel". Then the German executive, who apparently was an expert on river fish but also knew a lot about ocean fish too, apparently he said that in Germany they have one called "nine-eye eel", which Barb didn't know either, an' I joked to her later, after she got home at about three in the morning, "that's one in the eye for Japan", but she didn't get that either.

'Anyway, so that night after dinner and after the German executive guy left, Iemoto took Barb to the hotel at the top of Mt Hiei, where he apparently always kept a suite room for his disposal, or whatever. She told me she had been there before with him too. But she said he said he wasn't in the mood for sex because he was tired or whatever, or maybe, like, he just forgot to pop a little blue pill down his eel, I mean *with* his eel, but he asked her, apparently, to take off all her clothes and stand by the window. He wanted to see the outline of her body against the nighttime lights of Kyoto or something, I dunno, it's something to do with old men and what turns them on, I reckon. They say it's like trying to pick up a juicy piece of raw fish with chopsticks made out of old rope.

'Anyway, so apparently Iemoto confessed to her then, because he said he trusted her as much as he did Lonnie Kipsky, that he had heaps of businesses around the world, even a casino somewhere, which is illegal in Japan. He said, "Tea is my elegance, but in Japan all elegance relies on decay and corruption, the kind of corruption that erodes the perfect beauty of an object and displays its ugliness at the same time".

'Barb seemed to be really moved by this when she explained it to me, but it's all a bit too esoteric for me, I mean, I was brought up on a cattle station outside Canowindra in New South Wales, so elegance is something that passes me right by, but, so Iemoto went on, like, "It's something I learned from my wife's father. Gold doesn't tarnish, but beneath its surface is smeared a bright red layer. It's blood. The blood of others. That's what makes it beautiful. Right below the surface of stillness is constant motion … a hair's breadth beneath the serene comfort of tranquility is brutality, violence and pain. You know, Barbara, your grandfather understood that. I think that's why we were so close to each other. Even in the prisoner-of-war camp in Siberia we were close. We were both slaves then, slaves to a war that debased everyone forced to take part in it. Your grandfather was amazing. He told me then that he would go back to Germany and make a fortune, that he would never allow himself to be debased again. I was amazed at his strength, even though we were both forced to handle radioactive uranium that was eventually going to make its way into bombs that might fall on Germany and Japan one day, for all we knew at the time. It was your grandfather who gave me the strength to remake my life once I got back home to Japan. He went into coffee, and I into tea.

That always amused him no end. It was our experience as prisoners of war that inspired us to go back and get on top, never to allow others to force us into such demeaning, painful and inhumane situations again".

'Barb told me that she had been standing naked in front of the window while he spoke to her sitting on the bed dressed in the formal Japanese gear he had worn to the dinner that night in Gion. He stopped talking, rose from the bed and walked up to her. She said for some reason she felt scared, but she couldn't tell me why. Maybe she felt funny that he had been talking about her grandfather, who she really loved. After all, he was the one who made it possible for her to go to Kyoto. But she did what he said and stood by the window with no clothes on. Barb has a great body, I mean, almost perfect, not that I've seen her, I mean, like that, but her boobs are beautiful and she had a tiny little waist and really nice hips and bum an' everything.

'Anyway, so he stood in front of her and then went down on his knees and put his two hands around her and onto her bum. He put his face right up to her and asked her to spread her legs, I mean, stand with her legs apart. Then suddenly she said to me she felt disgusted, disgusted with herself and with him, like he was using her body to prove to himself that all beauty had a kind of, not ugliness, I mean just something wild inside it, something that was natural and not fashioned at all, because to him all elegance was really just a, like, formality, a ceremony with set artificial moves and poses.

'Yeah, that's it. It was to see the real beauty behind the artifice, if that's the word. It was obvious to her that that's what was in his mind, whether he knew it or not himself. He was using her as an object, getting close to her because he saw her on the outside as one of his little objects, an all-white and smooth-skin object, something he could put his hands all over and put up to his lips and lose himself in and feel like he was doing something real for once, unpractised, free.

'And she said to me then, "At that instant I wanted to leave there immediately. I realised that what I had left Germany for and what I had come to Kyoto for was all false, that the tea ceremony and

Japanese traditions and all that elegance people go on and on about in this country is just *Scheisse*, shit! It's like a little round pat of horseshit in the sun, Bunny. The surface of his elegance is smooth and perfect, but if you go close up to it and break it apart you find the centre to be soft and runny and stinking of what it is—*Scheisse*. That's what his elegance was. And oh yes, he knew it! He knew it all along, better than anyone, since the time he got back to Japan after the war. He knew that if he could only embrace it, embrace the shit ceremony, and sell it to Japanese people and to the world as beauty and elegance, he would be a kind of emperor in his own world. That's why he married his wife. To get to her money. He didn't care where that money came from. He is no better than those Japanese and Germans who sent millions of innocent young men to their deaths in battle. I am being used, Bunny, used by this man so that he can continue to think of himself as the creator of beauty, as the emperor of elegance".

'She apparently then shoved his hands off her, grabbed him by the Art Nature hairpiece that he wore and jerked his head away from her. The hairpiece stayed on despite the jerk. I reckon the Japanese make the best hairpieces anywhere an' that they could really market them around the world if they wanted to. So, she got dressed and walked out on him. Apparently he just stood at the window looking out over his beloved old city, a city that lay at his feet in more ways than one. He didn't say a word to her. He didn't even turn around once when she left.

'Two days later there was a terrible fire at the school and the old teahouse an' stuff burnt to the ground. Everyone knew that it was caused by Lonnie Kipsky and his boyfriend from Arizona who had nothing at all to do with tea but was living with Lonnie in the school anyway. The next morning the police arrived, but by then Lonnie and his boyfriend had already departed Kansai Airport for Los Angeles. The cause of the fire was listed as "spontaneous combustion" and no one was legally blamed for it. That way Iemoto got all the insurance money and the massive sympathy of the Japanese people he held in the palm of his hand like his precious little tea bowls.

'All of us in the Daidai-Kai had to go around the neighbourhood and to officials in the fire department and bow our heads in shame. Even though it was officially put down as caused by spontaneous combustion, we were still made to feel we were guilty and responsible. It's funny because the real people whose lit joint left on the tatami caused the fire were by then time zones away from Japan. Barb refused to apologise to everyone for the fire an' Iemoto couldn't force her, not after what happened at the hotel on Mt Hiei. She left for Germany a few days after that.

'That was four months ago now. I expected that I wouldn't hear from her again. I think she wanted to put Japan behind her, and that would mean cutting all ties with the past. But she did send me a mail with a selfie on Christmas Eve, taken at one of those Christmas markets they have in Germany. It's really so exotic for me because I associate Christmas with scorching heat an' picnics on the beach at Coogee, where I was living with my boyfriend Eric, a fourth-generation Chinese Australian, before we broke up and I came to Kyoto kinda, I mean, on the rebound, I reckon.

'Barb wrote that she spends a lot of time wandering around Hamburg's parks and watching families eating sausages and potato salad and drinking beer. I think she's withdrawn even further into herself, because she went on to write "They are so fucking noisy and gross it makes me sick. I don't want to hear them. I don't want to watch them. They are the picture of ugliness". I wrote her back that it was a pretty good description of Australians too.

'I wonder where she'll go next. She obviously isn't going to stay in Hamburg, and she's not coming back here, that's for sure. There's nothing for her here. She'll have to, like, find somewhere else, somewhere where she can seek out that beauty and harmony and quiet elegance she so desperately needed without going so deep into it that she loses herself. I guess it's a little like walking on mud, or something worse.

'As for me, well, I had to look for a new flat mate. This old place is much too big for me and the rent that Iemoto is charging me is exorbitant. I make a fair bit of money teaching English to preschoolers, but it doesn't leave me much for myself at the end of the month. I want to save up so that I can go on holiday to Thailand or Guam or somewhere like that. I don't miss Canowindra or Coogee at all. I've seen the pats of horseshit lying in the sun in the outback and the mindless idiots who just sit in the sun on the beach until their skin turns into cracked leather. There's nothin' beautiful or elegant about that either. It's just all part of the landscape of the culture, I reckon.

'I'm not plannin' on quitting tea, though I don't buy into all that shit that Barb was taken in by. It's just something to do. That's all it is. Better than lying on your belly under the sun all day long with a paperback you don't read. That's meaningless in my book.

'Being here still has some meaning to my life. I just don't know how to put the meaning into words.

'It's just as good being here as being anywhere, I reckon.'

Mrs Matsui

It was an open secret in my husband's course on modern Japanese literature at Smith College in the 1980s that his inspiration came not directly from the sensual prose and poetry of Japan but from his absolute devotion to me.

I sat in his class, his alter ego in more ways than one, front row centre. Not merely his thoughts but the very looks on his face reflected mine. I was, even then, white-maned when seen from the back, but I could throw an eagle's eye on all his little girls by swivelling about in my seat in the blink of an eye. I finished his sentences when the occasion warranted, spelling out the low and the high, the wicked and the good, the imperceptible colour of Japanese aesthetics that Americans could not know.

I walked diagonally across the Quad by his side, enveloping his fingers in mine, cold rungs in my fist that they were. His soft yet formal Japanese profile moved in perfect outline against the old bricks, a casual Japanese ink brush stroke on a permanent liver-red backdrop. And when his little girls, eager beavers, came towards us and greeted him, I made sure that he gazed at them full on, without the customary Japanese aversion of the eye.

The most luscious and voluptuous of them did merit a good looking over. I never denied him that pleasure. After having passed them, he would glance over his shoulder, on my side needless to say, and imagine himself fondling those wonderful American ballooned backsides. After all, such an imagination is truly Japanese ... only a

Japanese man can fondle with his eyes and feel relieved.

'The Obsession with Backsides in the Literature of Yasunari Kawabata' was an admirable and valid lecture topic, and one that my husband did ample justice to.

But his gaze always turned forward again, his palm suddenly sweating in mine, no doubt in reaction to the bobbing spheres that had disappeared up the steps of the library. I would then take out my silk Japanese handkerchief and wipe his palm for him, smirking benevolently at his little sin. Sometimes, if the girl had been particularly mouth watering, I would hold the back of his hand up and rub his knuckles against the fine strands of my long white hair. He appreciated that no end.

I loved my husband. He was the greatest genius in the university faculty. I was convinced of that. For that reason alone, I knew, we could never return to Japan. Japan is a country that rejects geniuses.

Oh, my husband and I did not mind in the least being despised in Japan. It is natural to be despised when you are innately superior to those around you. But neither of us would ever tolerate being ignored. The worst thing about Japanese people is that they ignore those of superior gifts. They find comfort solely in mediocrity … generally their own.

Each year saw some ten to twelve young Smith women sit his course. These young women were invariably the introverted type, drawn to the subtle passions that infuse Japanese literature, learning how not to express the heights of human emotion in a crude American fashion but rather to repress them, making their depressive ardour all the more painful and intense. In this way my husband's course produced, over the years, a bevy of young female enthusiasts, most of whom went to Japan to live after graduation, not returning to America for a long time, if at all.

It was in the eleventh year of our tenure at the university, 1986, that the incident occurred, due entirely to the presence in my husband's class of one Cheryl Druckwitz.

Cheryl Druckwitz was—I saw it the moment I set eyes on her—not the type of young American woman who should be attempting to unravel the intricate relationships described on the pages of modern Japanese literature. Her fingers were too thick for that, her inclinations entirely too frivolous and heated, and her mind too full of brazen agitation. How could a woman like that enter the delicate and sensuous world of Japanese femininity? I could have taught her how to do that … had I wished to.

She began the year with a careful but rashly conceived ploy: She sat directly behind me. Having a long back, she could easily see my husband over my head, and I was unable to glare at her as I did at the others with a simple twist of the neck.

From my husband's perspective there were two female heads, one atop the other; one with white hair—mine—and the other with jet black, hers. This visibly disconcerted him. Yet all he had to do to locate his bearings was to lower his gaze. I was willing and ready, at a second's notice, to throw him a line. I was the only person who could save my husband from the long embarrassments of silence. In the American classroom, even a short hesitation on the part of the professor invited derision from the students. Not so in Japan, where a well-timed silence could throw an inquisitive student straight back on her aggressive self.

The particular incident of aggression dished out by Cheryl Druckwitz began with a simple enough—what is often incorrectly termed an 'innocent'—question: 'Who do you think will be the first Japanese author to win a Nobel Prize for Literature after Yasunari Kawabata, Professor Matsui, and why?'

It may have been my imagination, but I did feel her wet breath striking the nape of my neck. Yet, I was not about to turn to her, oh no! She would have wanted that. I knew that she was asking her 'innocent' question in order to humiliate me. There was not the shadow of a doubt about that. Nevertheless, I fixed my eyes ahead, on my husband, smiling at him, nodding, yes, yes, go ahead, you may answer her, you know the answer, we have discussed this many times in the past, it's all right, do it.

But my husband simply stood on his little platform, peering fixedly above my head, curiously resembling a stunned pigeon on its perch. He could not utter a sound, despite the fact that I had given him the clear unspoken go-ahead to speak. I smiled once again at him, even more magnanimously than before. Still nothing. Not a word from his lips. His neck seemed locked in position, and he seemed unable to remove his sight from the face of the young American woman seated directly behind me.

The long pause was beginning to cause some commotion in the classroom. The other young women present were at a loss, not knowing how to interpret it. Suddenly, Cheryl Druckwitz broke the silence, blurting out a string of shameless questions …

'Well, Professor Matsui,' she said, 'if you can't answer that one, then maybe you can explain to us something about Junichiro Tanizaki. Why did he write a story about lesbians? I am, of course, referring to the novel *Manji*, which you assigned us to read. Tanizaki, I presume, was not a homosexual. I have read that he was actually quite the lecher. Can you explain his motives to us? Was he merely trying to exploit a scandalous issue, to make some money from a book about illicit sex? And, finally, what do you think personally of love and sex between two women, *Mrs Matsui*?'

I had been present in my front-row centre seat in all of my husband's courses during our entire tenure at Smith College, yet had never once been personally addressed by one of his students. Though I often thought in English, at that moment a single Japanese phrase resounded in my head. '*Haji o shire*! (Have you no shame?)' How dare she call attention to me!

My husband continued to stare at a point just above my head, standing as if bolted to the platform from head to toe by a stake. My smiles and nods were evidently not reaching him. There was nothing left for me to do but to leave him in that position, stand, face the class and speak for him.

'My husband has said on numerous occasions in this course,' I said, peering directly at Cheryl Druckwitz, 'that Yukio Mishima would have been the second Japanese Nobel laureate. In fact, to be precise, he had gone so far as to predict that in 1970. Unfortunately, Mr Mishima took his own life, thus somewhat ruling him out for the award. As to who will be the next laureate, both my husband and I have said on many occasions that there is no Japanese author today worthy of it. Japanese literature died sometime between the spring of 1981 and the summer of 1982. My husband wrote a brilliant article proving this in the literary journal "Umi", which folded and sunk in May 1984, further validating my husband's theory that Japanese people cannot face the truth.'

I turned momentarily back to my husband, who was standing in inert silence as before. He looked like a Bunraku doll abandoned by his manipulator.

'And as for your second question, *Ms* Druckwitz,' I continued, now showing her the full force of my Heian-period-like profile, 'may we turn your question to you yourself—are you yourself a lesbian, Ms Druckwitz? Is that why you are so concerned about the nature of personal relationships in Mr Tanizaki's novel? And may I remind you that this is a Japanese novel, not an American one. The emotions expressed in this novel are profound and delicate, perhaps a trifle too subtle and understated for someone brought up on "Bonanza", "Maverick" and "Leave it to Beaver" to *dig*.' (I had not majored at Waseda University in American pop culture for nothing.)

By the time I had finished addressing her, I was facing her square on. I had never even once so much as entertained the notion of dyeing my hair black or any other colour. My white hair was radiant, particularly from the back. I knew that its sheen would blind our students, as well as it did my husband, causing him to cast his eyes away from the dark, dull and, if I may say so, oddly proportioned ethnic face of Ms Cheryl Druckwitz.

My husband, gradually freeing himself from his motionless posture, like a puppet whose parts begin to stir again one by one, labouriously seated himself on the desk on the platform, cocked his head rather listlessly to one side, then to the other, shuffled some papers in his hands and turned a glazed look onto the young women in the room.

At that moment, as if by fate or chance—or, as it happens, a momentary mixture of the two—the bell tolled the end of the hour and the young women stood and left in single file. From among them only Cheryl Druckwitz remained. The three of us were alone in the room. She stared at us with a piercing gaze and said something totally flippant and outrageous.

'Why didn't you speak up, Keizo? Do you really need Mitsue to put words into your mouth for you?'

Having said this, she picked up her books and proceeded to walk out of the room without so much as a backward glance.

'How dare she call you by your given name!' I exclaimed to my husband. 'And where does she get the right to use my name? Sometimes I cannot stand this country. It is the women of this country who are the most vile. They have no sense of … of … balance in their lives, of, of decorum. They are simply bitches.'

I could not come to terms with hearing our given names coming from the lips of an American student. I was in every way a freethinking woman myself. I was deeply fond of my given name. Though it was originally written with the characters for 'light' and 'branch'—a branch of light, as if at birth I had appeared as a little ray of sunshine—I had, since my student days, taken to writing it in hiragana, using the ancient form of the letter 'e'. Such a rendering suited my poetic, gentle and quintessentially feminine nature.

Having heard my name and my husband's spoken with such derision by an American student, I felt as if both of us had been defiled, that something precious and uniquely Japanese had been made banal, and by being made banal, had been violently wrested from us. This form of uncalled-for intimacy was intolerable. We Japanese adore intimacy, but only when it is called for.

My husband came down with an inexplicable fever that night. It lasted for some ten days. I had considered taking over his lectures, but we decided to cancel the classes instead, seeing as, in any case, the university was approaching its Easter break.

On those chilly Massachusetts spring nights, while my husband lay in bed, I took to walking along Elm St., wondering if two graduates of Smith College, Nancy Reagan and Sylvia Plath, had passed there before me. I had a vision of them holding hands and occasionally exchanging intimate glances.

I stopped in at the bar in the Hotel Northampton on King St. I enjoyed observing earnest American students from my vantage point at a corner table. I was never looked at myself. I may as well not have been there. I returned to that bar every night, delighting in my invisibility and the keen insight of my silent observations.

One night, about a week after my husband fell ill, a young woman whom I had never seen before approached my table.

'May I sit here?' she asked.

'Of course you may,' I answered.

She sat herself down, folded her hands on the table and looked at me in the saucy and vaguely obnoxious manner of an American undergraduate. Finally she spoke …

'You're Mrs Matsui, aren't you, Professor Matsui's wife.'

'Yes. You are not one of our students, though. I do not recognise you.'

'Oh, your husband is known by a lot more people than just his own students, Mrs Matsui. He's famous on campus.'

'I see. Well, he is very brilliant, you know. He could have taken up a position at Tokyo University, but, well, he would not fit in there. Tokyo University is a place for, how shall I put this, for mental robots.'

'Mrs Matsui, I do not know if you are aware of this, but your husband has the reputation on campus of being, how shall I put this, a ladies' man?'

'A ladies' man? I do not understand this colloquialism. He has a superb grasp of womanhood.'

'Precisely. He's a skirt chaser, Mrs Matsui. A man who goes after a lot of women. He is very good looking, your husband. He is considered a real sexpot at Smith, you know, a heartthrob, kind of.'

'I do not think that you are correct. What is your name?'

'Sandy. Sandy Glickman.'

'And do you know my husband personally, Sandy Glickman? Has my husband been chasing your skirt? Has your heart been throbbing, as you say, because of my husband?'

'Me? No. But I am a close friend of Cheryl Druckwitz's. I think you know her. In fact, Mrs Matsui, I think that you really do know what has been going on between her and your husband. You must know. God knows, everyone else does.'

'Nothing has been "going on", as you say. My husband is ill. He is at home.'

'That's now. What about last year when Cheryl went to his office in November to talk to him about his course? You were in New York, or something, weren't you? Giving a talk at the Japan Society or something? Mrs Matsui?'

The pianist, a short dark-skinned man with a full rounded moustache and shiny slicked-back hair, stood up from a high stool at the bar, walked to the piano and played a loud chord before sitting down.

'I'm back, folks, and just to remind you about an old film with that cool dude Humphrey Bogart, here's a little song for all you beautiful lovers.'

He started to play 'As Time Goes By'.

'Well, I think I'll be going,' said Sandy Glickman, pushing her seat back. 'I heard that you have been coming here every night and sitting alone at this table. Maybe you're searching for something too, just like your husband, Mrs Matsui.'

She left my table and started to walk away from me.

'Wait, I said. What … I mean, where is Cheryl Druckwitz now?'

She stopped in the middle of the room, turned around and rested her fingertips on a tabletop.

'Huh? Oh, Cheryl's in the hospital, Mrs Matsui. As if you didn't know!'

She had said the last words loudly, to make sure that I could hear them above the sound of the song.

'The hospital? Why?'

'Because of her face, Mrs Matsui. Because somebody—she is not saying who, not even to the police—because somebody slit her left cheek from her jaw to her temple with a serrated kitchen knife.'

She closed her fist and brought it down with considerable force on the tabletop, turned to the door and walked out.

I felt as if I had been struck by her fist. Her plain words, spoken with such unconcealed malice—'as if you didn't know'—had hit me hard. Someone was grabbing my throat, squeezing it with a constant force, allowing me to breathe only in gasps. I bolted up, feeling faint, and braced myself by resting my knuckles on the top ridge of my chair. My white hair was a mask covering my entire face.

How could I possibly have known what had happened to Cheryl Druckwitz? I knew nothing about this woman. For all I knew she had inflicted the wound on her own cheek. Any woman who was capable of humiliating my husband in public with such impudent questioning—uttering his given name as if it were hers to call up at will—was surely capable of taking a knife in hand, piercing her flesh with it and defacing herself. I would not be held responsible for the naive actions of my husband's misdirected students!

I believed in my heart that my husband was not capable of anything more than gazing at the curvaceous bodies of the young women on campus. I had been in New York in November of the previous year, remaining in the city for a day after my lecture to see a film version of *Anna Karenina*. It was unimaginable that my husband would take advantage of my absence to do more with these young women than let his eye run over their clothed bodies. Unimaginable.

On my way home from the hotel bar I stopped in at the university medical centre, enquiring as to whether a Cheryl Druckwitz was a patient there. She was.

'But it is long past visiting hours now,' the petite Filipina nurse said to me.

'I am the wife of her professor of Japanese literature, Professor Keizo Matsui. You may have heard of him. I have here in my purse an essay which my, well, husband has corrected and wishes to return to Ms Druckwitz. I think that the result might cheer her up.'

'Oh, how very kind of you. I guess it's okay. She is down the corridor in Room 54. You will see her name on the door. Thank you.'

I stood at the door to Room 54. A little plastic name plaque, not unlike the nameplates that Japanese display on a pillar by the front gate of their houses, read 'C. Druckwitz'. I opened the door without knocking. A chill ran down my spine, and my legs were shaking.

There were four beds in the room, but only one was occupied. Cheryl was asleep, or appeared to be. I quietly shut the door behind me and approached her bed. As I did, almost as part of the same motion, she sat up. We stared at each other for some time without saying a word. I held tightly onto the soft plastic curtain that hung around her bed.

'I heard about this from your friend, Sandy Glickman,' I finally said. 'Who did this to you?'

She paused for what must have been a full minute, not taking her eyes off me. Then she took hold of the bandage covering her cheek and slowly removed it. Underneath was a raised brownish red scar of about one centimetre's width running the entire length of the left side of her face.

'Who did this to me?' she asked. 'Why, you did, Mrs Matsui. You did this to me.'

She was squinting at me. When Japanese squint they look friendly. Their eyes smile. But when an American squints at you, you receive nothing but scorn.

'Oh, don't gasp in horror, Mrs Matsui. And please do remove your hand from your own cheek. The gesture reeks too much of empathy. I won't tell the police that you did it. I want to spare Keizo the embarrassment.'

'But of course I did not do this to you,' I said. 'Where did I do it then?'

'Where? In my kitchen, Mrs Matsui.'

'But I have never been in your kitchen.'

'No, I guess not. But Keizo has. Lots of times. I guess I just thought you two were inseparable, that's all.'

I did not get home that night until past midnight. My husband was sitting on the sofa in the living room watching a rerun of 'The Lone Ranger'.

'You've never been this late before, Mitsue,' he said with a wan smile. 'Is everything all right?'

I asked him if he was feeling better.

'Yes,' he replied. 'I think so. I think I'm nearly back to my old self.'

I never asked my husband if Cheryl Druckwitz had visited him in his office in November of the previous year, or if he had ever set foot in her, or any other young American woman's, kitchen. He, for his part, did not seem anxious to know where I had been during the nights of his illness. I certainly wasn't following in the footsteps of Nancy Reagan or Sylvia Plath. There are only two types of American woman in existence and they represent them. There are no American women like me, and no amount of the study of our literature would ever allow them to be.

Cheryl Druckwitz did not return to Smith after the Easter break. My husband and I did not hear from her, or of her, after that. I did, however, run into Sandy Glickman in the early autumn of 1987 at a sandwich bar on West St. My husband and I found ourselves standing beside her at the counter. The man behind the counter looked at the three of us and said, 'All right, who's next?'

'No, you go ahead,' said Sandy Glickman to my husband, looking straight through me. 'You were here before me.'

That was all. Not a trace of recognition. Not a word about her close friend, Cheryl Druckwitz, or about her having met me—no acknowledgment that our paths in life had ever crossed.

In 1994, Kenzaburo Oe was awarded the Nobel Prize for Literature. I had read only one book by him, *A Personal Matter*. It's about a man who is unfaithful to his wife while she is having his baby. Such a story is totally revolting, and I saw no need to read other books by that man.

That same year, my husband and I returned to Japan for good. He became a professor of American literature at a prestigious women's college outside Kobe. We live in a spacious apartment in Nishinomiya. I teach Western cooking twice a week at home to a group of highly motivated Japanese women. I have gone back to signing my name with the two characters for 'light' and 'branch'. It's more dignified and formal that way.

While I may have somewhat softened my views on life, cut my hair short and dyed it a light brown, I have stuck firmly to one principle: I never discuss any aspect of my relationship with my husband to anyone. To do so would be demeaning ... to him, if not to me. I am a woman who knows how to keep everything to herself.

Sometimes it seems to me that we never left Japan, that even when we were in America we were living in Japan all the while, a Japan with a culture that so few—my husband and I among them—remain intimate with.

Our Father

HAVING GROWN UP AS AN ONLY CHILD YOU CANNOT IMAGINE MY happiness upon discovering that I had a sister ... well, a half-sister. But that didn't matter to me. A half-sister was better than no sister at all. I am usually a lonely girl who lives on daydreams. Now I had something real that I could really dream about, day and night.

I never would have found out about her existence had I not uncovered a letter. It was written in such small script that I needed a magnifying glass to read it. It had been kept for what must have been years in an old shoebox underneath my mother's bed.

Mother had gone to work at the factory one day, leaving me on my own. I had a chest cold and was staying away from school. I chased our cat, Rembrandt, into mother's room and found him snuggling up to the dusty cardboard box that was coming apart in two of its corners. It had no ribbon around it. I dragged it from under the bed onto mother's worn Persian carpet and carefully removed the lid.

The first thing that struck my eye was an old letter in an unsealed envelope sitting on top of a small carved teak jewellery box. I removed the letter, written on waxy semi-transparent paper, and unfolded it. I took it to my desk where I kept my magnifying glass. It was a love letter to mother written in broken Bahasa Indonesia, and it made me blush. It ended with these words ...

'I regret my daughter never grow up see me. One day please tell to

59

her about me. Please.'

It was signed: 'With love, Masahiko' … except that the last letter of the word for 'love'—*cinta*—was left out, so it was like 'lov', though I knew what he meant.

I slipped the letter back into its envelope, replaced the lid on the box and pushed it under the bed until it came to rest against Rembrandt's paw. He raised his head on a weary angle, threw me a lazy look, yawned and fell promptly back to sleep.

That night I was unusually silent at supper. When mother asked me what the matter was I blurted out that I had read her letter. I fully expected her to erupt in anger at me, but she merely smiled. Her eyes welled with tears. She reached across the table and took both my hands in hers.

'Wiwy,' she said, 'your father was not an Indonesian. He was a Japanese named Masahiko Sato. He may still be alive. I don't know. He only ever wrote me one letter and that was fifteen years ago. I lived with your father for four years, Wiwy.'

Mother gripped my hands tightly as she broke down and sobbed. I walked around to her and stood beside her. She rested her head against my side.

That is when I took it upon myself to find my father. I wrote a letter to him in my best English and sent it to the address that was on the back of his letter's envelope. The address was in Japanese, so I cut it out, pasted it on the face of the envelope of my letter to him, and added the word 'Jepang' along the bottom.

Some months passed, and though I had put my father out of my mind I noticed that a change had taken place in my mother's behaviour. She was often drowsy after supper. She would fall asleep in front of the television then abruptly wake up, exclaiming, 'I haven't been asleep … I've seen the entire program.' At night I could hear her crying in bed. Rembrandt sensed this change too. He left my bed, where he had slept since he was a kitten, for mother's.

One day a letter arrived from Japan. It was written in English on pink paper decorated on top with a cartoon drawing of a cute dog in a little suit and hat. Beside the dog were the letters 'Snoopy'. I guess that Snoopy must be the Japanese word for 'dog'.

The father of a friend from school came to my house to help translate the letter for me.

'This letter is not from Mr Sato,' he said. 'It is from a young woman named Rieko Sato. She appears to be Mr Sato's daughter.'

As he read the letter out loud, mother and I held hands so tightly that our knuckles were white by the end of it. This is what Rieko Sato wrote …

'My father, Masahiko Sato, died last year of lung cancer. My mother and I live together in a town called Senri, which is in Osaka prefecture. My mother did not know that father had another child in Jakarta. It has come as a big shock to her. But I am very happy to know you, Wiwy-san. You are my only sister! Please come and live with me in Japan! Your sister, Rieko.'

RIEKO TELLS HER STORY

I CANNOT SAY THAT THE NEWS OF MY FATHER'S OTHER CHILD IN Indonesia was entirely welcome. Father had gone to that country in 1976 to work as chief engineer on a bridge construction project. He had previously helped design and build some of the walkways at the Osaka Expo in 1970. Father had stayed away for four years, and during that time mother saw him only once. It was on that visit back home that I was conceived. By the time he returned to Japan I was two, so I really don't remember missing him before then.

After the letter from my half-sister Wiwy arrived from Indonesia, mother started to act strangely. She would go to her room shortly after dinner and not come out till the morning. One night after she had gone to sleep I peeked into her room. She was asleep on top of the bed with her clothes on. A half-empty bottle of Suntory brandy stood under her bedside lamp. The lamp had been left on, and mother's body was bathed in a soft yellow light. She was holding the brandy bottle's cap between her bent fingers.

I gently pulled her fingers apart and screwed the cap back on to the bottle. Then I covered her with a blanket and turned off the bedside lamp.

WIWY CONTINUES

I was so excited to hear the news of Rieko, my Japanese sister. I told all my friends at school. Some called me a braggart, but I think that was only the ones who were jealous of me.

I wrote another letter to her telling her absolutely everything about myself. I took it to my friend's father and asked him to translate it properly into English for me.

'I can't translate this,' he said. 'It's forty-five pages long.'

'Well,' I said, taking the thick wad of pages back from him, 'can't you just cut it down a page or two? You can leave out the stuff about when I was really little. It's so important to me that my sister knows as much about me as possible. We have so much time to catch up on.'

My friend's father sighed, shrugged his shoulders and promised me that he would do his best.

Not long after that mother fell ill. She had to see the doctor once a week. She refused to tell me what was wrong with her, but I sensed that it was something serious. She seemed so sad and tired all the time.

One of my friends—well, I had always considered her one of my friends—was spreading the rumour that the only reason why my mother and I lived in a big house was because my father had sent a lot of money from Japan to buy it for us. I asked mother if this was true but all she said was, 'I begged him to stay with me in Jakarta. He held you in his arms, Wiwy. You were three so you don't remember. But you just cried and cried too. He left the next day for his home in Japan.'

Rieko is so lucky. She knew our father.

RIEKO CONTINUES

I CAN'T BELIEVE THE LETTER I RECEIVED FROM MY INDONESIAN half-sister. It was thirteen pages long! She wrote me about herself, her mother, her friends at school and how much she enjoys cooking, doing embroidery, dyeing and making her own clothes and clothes for her mother. I took her letter to my school and read it out loud in English to my classmates.

'She's so poor,' I said. 'She has to make her own dresses. You wouldn't believe it's 1995 now if you just read this letter. I bet she doesn't have her own computer or even a Game Boy!'

We all laughed, because her letter sounded like it was written by a dirt-poor farm girl in Tohoku before the war that the teacher once made us read.

'What can you possibly write her back?' asked my best friend, Motoko, as we played together in my room on my new Sega Saturn game console. 'You two have nothing at all in common.'

'Yeah. We only have one thing in common. But that's not really a big thing for me. It's more of a big thing for my mum, though. Hey, you're being mean! Mot-chan, you're too fast for me in pressing the buttons. Be fair!'

After that we went shopping at Umeda where I bought this amazing Moschino scarf. We met this American guy, too, at KFC. His name was Don and he boasted that he had his own BMW, but both Mot-chan and I knew he was lying.

WIWY ENDS HER STORY

A YEAR HAD PASSED SINCE I FOUND MY FATHER'S LOVE LETTER TO my mother in the shoebox beneath her bed, and I had written seven letters to Rieko in Japan during that time.

Mother had to leave home to stay at the hospital. When I was visiting her, as I tried to do every day, my auntie who was there offered to come and live with me. But I said that I was already eighteen and could live by myself. Mother was proud of me. Though she had completely lost her voice after the operation, she nodded her head over and over again and squeezed my hand.

Not long after that, another letter arrived from Japan. It was only the second one that I ever received from my half-sister. This one was in Japanese, not English, and I took it to the Japanese embassy in the city hoping that someone there would be able to translate it for me. I skipped school that day. It took me nearly two hours by bus to get to the embassy.

I waited on line in front of a counter for a long time. But I was turned away by a young Japanese woman sitting on the other side of the plate glass barrier stuck to the counter. Apparently it was the line for people who wanted to visit Japan. The word 'Visa' was written on a sign stuck to the glass, but I didn't know what 'Visa' meant.

The embassy closed at noon for ninety minutes. I walked around among some very big buildings. It was the first time that I had come into the city by myself and I hadn't brought any food for myself to eat for lunch.

I returned to the embassy at 1:25 and entered the lift on the ground floor. Just as the door was shutting to go up to the embassy, I saw the young woman from behind the counter running towards the lift. I thrust my hand between the doors and they opened automatically.

'*Terima kasih* (Thank you),' she said.

I was so surprised to hear a foreigner speaking Bahasa Indonesia that I couldn't say a word to her. But as the lift ascended I realised that my chance had come. I am usually a very shy girl, but I quickly took Rieko's letter from my backpack and held it out to her. She gave me a puzzled look. Not knowing what to say to her I simply lowered my head and stared at the floor of the lift.

We stood together outside the lift for a moment. The young woman spoke to me in my language.

'This letter is from Rie Sato of Senri, Osaka. She says to you here, "Please never write to me again. I do not want to know you. Your letters made my mother sick. If you write to me ever again, my mother will get even sicker. Please forget your Japanese half-sister forever. Goodbye". That's the last word of the letter. In Japanese it is *sayonara*.'

She handed me back the letter, pressed some numbered buttons beside the side door to the embassy office and stepped in. When the door opened I could see a line of about thirty-five or forty people waiting for her in front of the counter.

I put my Japanese half-sister's letter into my backpack and stepped back into the lift. Once on the street I stood for a long time in front of the tall modern building that the Japanese embassy was in. The face of the building was all windows. They were reflecting the grey sky from one edge of the building to the other. I think I was in kind of a daze.

Many businessmen in dark suits were brushing by me in a rush. Sometimes their sleeves touched my shoulder, but they didn't apologise. I started running in the direction of the bus stop, holding onto my backpack with one hand behind my back so that it wouldn't bounce up and down.

I was wearing my best dress that day. It was a yellow cotton dress with smocking across the front that I made specially for mother's birthday. I was so glad that I hadn't got it dirty, because I wanted to wear it to visit mother in the hospital the next day. I always wanted to look my very best for her. I just hoped that she could come home so that I could look after her. I can look after her better than anyone else at that hospital ever can.

Rembrandt misses mother too. He has slept on her bed every night since she left.

I once even found him under the bed, sleeping right up against her old shoebox with the torn corners.

Outside Mesquite

As a child I used to count them. They seemed to have no beginning and no end. I make a vow, standing here in this searing heat, on top of a boulder like an upturned frypan: *I will kill him.* He doesn't deserve to go on living.

I have stopped now at one hundred. A hundred train cars, and they are still coming, one after another. The train stretches from one horizon to the other, and for all I know now, beyond.

I cannot wait until the long train passes in front of me and disappears before I move. I will not be a statue on a rock in the middle of nowhere. I will return to *his* house, his little hacienda, as he calls it, and stick a knife in his neck, under his chin, through his mouth, nose, and if the knife is long enough, his eyes. I must make sure to destroy his eyes above all.

You may ask how it came about that such a mild-mannered and gentle young man as I am would be entertaining such gruesome thoughts … I was going to call my thoughts 'extreme', but they are not extreme if justifiable to the mind.

Some of the train cars are carrying passengers, and I can see their faces interrupted by the metal between windows as they flash by me. Car after car, and all the faces appear the same. My own face, in reflection, is broken up as well, an image in frames of a film advancing more slowly than is normal.

Ah, normal! That has been my problem: I am normal. I am completely and totally and unequivocally normal.

The train is still going forward, and I am walking back towards his little hacienda. I shift my grey Armani suit jacket off my shoulder and toss it deftly onto a cactus, and wipe my brow with my patterned, red Missoni necktie. I am finding it hard to breathe. The radio this morning said it would be a hundred and twelve degrees in Mesquite … in the shade. This is the desert outside Mesquite … in the sun. I keep walking. The man on the radio said that July is the hottest month here. The red necktie is gone now too, coiled somewhere by the side of the road.

He would be with Mayumi now, in bed. They have finished making love, and he is cupping one hand around his whiskey glass and the other over her breast. There is no sheet over them. I picture myself slitting his throat, in an uppercut, while he is naked next to her. I want her to see what I am capable of.

IT SEEMS LIKE AGES SINCE I WAS SENT TO TOKYO BY AL KLEINMAN, 'art broker and connoisseur', to set up an office for his New York company, Greenwich Art Investments. But it was only June … a mere two weeks ago.

'Japan is more like Europe than you might suppose, Ben,' he had said to me. 'Don't be put off by all that trumped-up mysteriousness the Japanese dish out.'

I had graduated from Brigham Young University with a degree in Business Administration, but had spent two years in Leiden getting a Master's Degree in modern Dutch painting. The only thing I knew about Japanese art was that their woodblock prints had influenced Van Gogh.

'Take a good look at this name card, Ben. When you get to Tokyo, contact Takeo Yamaji, president of Yamaji Trading Company. He is one of Japan's foremost collectors of contemporary art. Get on his good side and we are in business in Japan.'

It was early July when I felt myself settled enough in Tokyo to visit

Takeo Yamaji, whose offices were in the Aoyama Twin Towers not far from the Oakwood Residence I was staying in. A downpour of rain had ended abruptly with a few claps of thunder, and by the time I set out on foot, the air was like a dense whitish curtain hanging just over the tops of buildings.

A uniformed receptionist at Yamaji Trading Company ushered me into a large empty waiting room, leaving me alone there. She returned some moments later with a cup of hot green tea, said what I recognised from my conversation book to mean 'Please wait a little while', and once again left me to myself.

After some time, a stout man in his mid-sixties entered the room, followed by a beautiful young Japanese woman. Mr Yamaji spoke Japanese, which the woman interpreted for him in fluent, slightly accented English.

'I'm sorry that I don't speak English, Mr Rush. But Kitabatake here does. Are you someone who is familiar with things Japanese?'

I apologised to him for my ignorance of Japanese art.

'All the better,' he said. 'No preconceptions. We Japanese prefer Westerners who come to us as a *hakushi*.'

'One moment, please,' said Ms Kitabatake. 'I must look up *hakushi*. Ah yes. It's tabula rasa.'

'Well, that's me!' I blurted out, inadvertently sounding like a teenager.

Mr Yamaji smiled, no doubt pleased to be dealing with someone who seemed unperturbed by his own naivete. He picked up a piece of pottery that was on the low table between us.

'Look at this, Mr Rush. This is a piece of Oribe pottery. Do you see this thick green drip of glaze?'

'Yes.'

'Erotic, wouldn't you say?'

I felt myself blushing. Yet, Ms Kitabatake, translating, had said the word 'erotic' straight to my face, without so much as blinking an eye.

'Look, let's get down to business. I like Americans, Ben. I am going to call you Ben, is that all right?'

'Sure. Thank you.'

'I'm Takeo, but you can call me Tak-e. And she is Mayumi.'

'Nice to meet you,' I said, surprised by my own awkward bashfulness.

'I have known Al Kleinman for over forty years, ever since we were students at Doshisha University in Kyoto. I trust him. And that is why I trust you, Ben. I have a proposition for you. Do you know the British artist Will Hailsham?'

'Of course I do. Mr Kleinman bought one of his works through Christie's last year.'

'I know. He was bidding for me. I am most keen to own a few more. They don't come on the market very often. I want to go right to the source. Do you know where he lives?'

'I think so. Somewhere in Arizona or somewhere like that.'

'That's right. Nevada, outside a place called Mesquite. I want you to go there next week, meet him and befriend him. I will introduce you by email. You decide what works I should buy and at what price. Just tell Al and I'll transfer the money to his account. How's that for a proposition, eh?'

'Wow, amazing. I never thought I would be sent back to my own country so soon for business.'

'Your own country, yes, yes. Oh, and I want you to take Mayumi with you. Is that all right with you?'

'Why … yes, of course.'

I found myself staring down at the glass-top table between us. Mr Yamaji held the piece of pottery, moving it round and round in his hands like a little wheel.

I walked out of the Twin Towers and onto the street. Crowds of elegantly dressed people were rushing by me and, for an instant, I couldn't place where I was.

WE WERE BESIDE EACH OTHER, IN BUSINESS CLASS SEATS, ON THE JAL plane to Los Angeles.

'Why did you choose to go into the art business?' Mayumi asked me. 'You seem like the scholarly type to me.'

'Well, my dad was an old friend of Mr Kleinman's, and he sort of wanted me to make a start in the business world.'

'But the art business is crass … and vulgar.'

I was shocked to hear Mayumi, who seemed to be so decorous and proper, say this.

'Crass? Is it? Isn't it about beauty?'

'Beauty?' she said, glancing out the window at a bank of white cloud that looked like the huge crest of a wave. 'Maybe there's still some beauty left in it. Who knows?'

She turned to look at me out of the corner of her eye and again fixed her sight on the clouds.

'How come you're, I mean, where did you learn such good English?'

'Me?' she said, still looking out the window. 'In Pennsylvania. I did a homestay for two years.'

'That must have been fun.'

'Fun? More like torture. Not a book in the house. No movies, no jokes, no talking at the table. They were like damn Pilgrims.'

'Well, not everyone in America is like that.'

'Yeah, I know.'

She was now staring straight into my eyes, not smiling. It wasn't an unfriendly look, just a look that I had no way of reading.

She is dozing now, I thought, and I can study her face and body all I want. Is she embarrassed to be going on a trip with an American man she hardly knows? She seems to be offering me warmth in one instant and a blank chill in another. She has a demure and distant quality, and yet there is something piercing … is it a wildness? … in her look. Extravagance, that's what she has, an extravagance of a contained kind that I have never encountered in any person or painting.

I was driving a Lexus that we rented in Las Vegas, heading for Mesquite. We crossed a railroad track and I did not notice the boulder that the next day I would be standing on, contemplating how I could kill Will Hailsham. Mayumi, a map over her lap, was guiding me.

'Turn left there, onto that dirt road,' she said, pointing ahead. 'It should be about three kilometres down that road.'

A few Joshua trees, some tumbleweed, a cloud of ochre dust churned up by the tyres of the Lexus as I turn onto the road … that's all I saw there.

'Are you tired?' I asked her.

'Nope. I snoozed on the plane from L.A. to Las Vegas.'

We came to what looked like an oasis, with a stand of palm trees, a large pond and an expanse of neatly cropped lawn. Along the edge of the lawn was a white pebbled driveway; and at the lawn's far edge a two-storey stucco house with curved black iron bars on the front door and windows, and a Spanish-tile roof so red that it hurt the eye.

I stopped the car before turning into the driveway.

'This is his house,' said Mayumi, folding the map and putting it in the glovebox.

'Yes, it is, I guess.'

Suddenly I found myself laying my right hand gently on her bare knee and saying her name.

'No. *Dame*! (Stop it!),' she said, pulling her pleated pink crepe skirt over her knees, opening the car door and, leaving it open, striding across the lawn.

I took my seatbelt off to reach her door and shut it. That is when I caught sight of the figure of a man standing in the front doorway, gripping the curved iron bars with both his hands.

Hailsham greeted us like long-lost friends, with a hug and a warm handshake. He offered us drinks and showed us into every room in his house. A Jackson Pollock in the living room; an Edward

Hopper in the den; a Winslow Homer in the dining room; and, the greatest surprise of all, a Norman Rockwell in the bedroom.

'It amuses me to have sex with Rockwell's rosy-cheeked innocent people staring down at me,' he said. 'Very American, wouldn't you say? The union of the prude and the crude.'

Mayumi, who had been studying the Rockwell, turned about, thrusting out her glass in a gesture to ask for more white wine.

'Why did you settle out here, Mr Hailsham?'

'I'm surprised it took you so long to ask me that, Ben,' he said, offering me a refill of wine, which I declined. 'Everyone asks me that. You know the real reason? We're not far from Virgin Valley here. I saw that on the map and I says to meself, "That's for me". After all, I grew up in Sheffield, mate, bleak, drab old Sheffield. Plenty of virgins there, but no open country like here. I like open things.'

After dinner and nightcaps, he sent Mayumi and me off to our bedrooms. He was sitting on a large Chesterfield sofa, staring into the empty fireplace. Above the mantel was a sketch by Whistler of a young Caucasian girl in a kimono holding a fan with butterflies painted on it. Only the butterflies had colour.

I SLEPT FOR OVER NINE HOURS, AND WHEN I AWOKE THERE SEEMED to be no one in the house. I called out.

'Mr Hailsham? ... Mayumi?'

I looked out through the barred windows onto the front lawn. Again they were not to be seen. I went into the kitchen. Through the kitchen window I caught sight of the two of them about to enter a small stucco building, like a converted garage, some distance from the house. Both Hailsham and Mayumi were staring down at the ochre dust as they walked. He held the door for her and she disappeared into a black rectangle.

'Mayumi reminds me so much of my wife, you know,' he had told us the night before. 'She was a Japanese, too. Look, Ben, why don't you write an article about me for my next catalogue. I'll give you all the tantalising details. You know, all that juicy stuff about artists. You yawn in my face and I'll yawn in yours. People hear that stuff and they think they understand the artist better for it. It's all so amusing.'

I walked out the kitchen door of the house towards the little building. It was not yet ten in the morning, yet the heat was already oppressive. I wiped sweat off my upper lip with the back of my hand.

Hailsham had left the door open, perhaps to keep the room inside cool, or perhaps—it actually occurred to me then—to draw me in.

I stood in the doorway. It took a moment for my eyes to become accustomed to the dim interior light. There were two rooms in the building. I could see Mayumi through the door to the far room, but I could not see him. I opened my eyes wide. Mayumi was just sitting herself down on a bridge chair in profile to me. She grasped the bottom of her blouse with both hands and pulled it over her head, removing it. She was not wearing a bra. She dropped her blouse to the floor, folded her hands in her lap and stared straight ahead. Her skin seemed to glow, catching and absorbing all the light that was there.

'How can she do this for him? He cannot force her to do this for him!'

I swayed in the doorway, maintaining my balance by pushing my raised palms up against the lintel.

Now *he* appeared in my line of sight. He held a paintbrush in his right hand. His left hand was on his chin. He let go of his chin and moved his hand towards her face. He felt her cheeks, nodding his head, then squeezed her jawbone with his thumb and index finger. His hand moved down onto her shoulder, tracing the line of her collarbone with his middle finger.

I gasped for a breath, gripping the lintel with all my might lest I fall backwards into the dust.

His hand moved further down. She was perfectly still, giving him that same cold unsmiling stare that she had given me. She was not resisting him. I whispered to myself, 'Push away his hand. Push away his goddamn hand!'

The tip of his index finger touched her right nipple. Then, with the hand that held the paintbrush, he fondled her left breast, rubbing the nipple with his thumb as if it was a coin that he was gently polishing.

For a moment there were only two textures in the world, that of the skin on the tip of his thumb and that on her nipple. I could see nothing else. Nothing else was catching the light that was in there. I had become an innocent observer, the invisible man in the next room in a painting by Vermeer, wanting to see something else but drawn against his will into seeing only one thing—the thing the artist was willing me to see.

I turned about and ran out of there, past the house, down the driveway, the Lexus all too bright to see, the palm trees and the pond that may as well not have been there now, back down the dirt road to the main highway, running, then slowing down, then running again.

I am stopped here. A train is on the tracks and I cannot cross them. I can't go ahead. I stand on a boulder and watch the train cars pass before me, seeing fragments of faces, one of them my own, flash in every window.

I start to retrace my steps while the train keeps going on. I am returning to the house. I wish to kill him. I will find them in bed together. He doesn't want to paint her portrait. That is so clear to me. He doesn't know the meaning of beauty. The only thing he understands is possession.

But I stop at the turnoff to the dirt road. I have no coat and no necktie. I am soaked to the bone, but there is no one there to see me like this. Not a soul. I am no longer in the picture.

I want to tell Mayumi that her body is being used by him, but I am stopped dead.

That is all I feel now, the need to tell her what is happening to her. That is the extent of my desire.

Rice

I CANNOT IMAGINE WHY YOU WOULD WANT TO LISTEN TO THIS, WHY anyone in the world now would take an interest in my story. What did you say your name was? Sachiko? Is that written with the character for 'happiness'? You see, I have not forgotten my Japanese altogether, not forgotten that I am a Japanese.

I have never been able to talk about myself in this country. Other immigrants could. When I had my first baby—Clark—I shared a room at Cedars of Lebanon Hospital with seven other women. They were Irish, Italian, German, Polish and African American, and all of them knew a thing or two about the others' nationality. They had some picture of it in their mind. But when they turned to me, instead of asking what Japanese life was like, they cocked their head and said, 'Oh, it's all so strange to us', and 'You are so different, how do you manage to live in America?'

No matter how many times I told them that I was born and raised in this country, they shook their head in amazement at my command of English.

My two boys, Clark and Ernie, grew up and went off. One became a professional sports car racer before retiring to Hawaii, the other joined the Navy. I never hear from them. Ernie … he's the one in the Navy … once played a little joke on me. He sent me two birthday cards at once. 'This is for this year and next year. Happy Birthdays, Mother.' Who knows, maybe he was trying to save on postage. I didn't hear from him for some years after that.

My husband, Jim Harrison, was a life insurance salesman who convinced everyone to buy a policy but never bought one himself. So, when he had a stroke and died in 1956, I had to go out and work, cleaning houses for rich people in Beverly Hills and Brentwood. Japanese women had a good reputation in those days. People saw us as silent, devoted and industrious. I suppose they were right.

I was a lucky Japanese American, I think you could say. During the war I was not sent to a camp, though we did have to leave California for fear of violence against me by people who called themselves 'ordinary Americans'. From January 1942 until November 1945 we lived in Cross Keys, Pennsylvania, a very small town populated mostly by Amish people. When we returned to L.A. we were given our house back, though the furniture we had left there had been sold off.

'What's a few tables and chairs?' said Jim, hugging me and the two boys when we stood for the first time after the war in our empty living room. 'I'm sorry that my country did this to you, Haruko.'

'It's mom's country, too,' said Clark, wrapping his arms around my waist.

'Yes and no,' I said.

'I won't let go of you until you say yes!' sobbed Clark.

When Jim died I wrote to my mother, who was living in Kameoka, near Kyoto, but she returned my letter with only one sentence written along the margin …

'I am not surprised that your husband died young because, thanks to you, your father also died before his time.'

She had underlined the words 'thanks to you'.

Mother was … she was … oh …

SACHIKO THE NURSE TAKES UP THE STORY

M RS H ARRISON DOZED OFF WHILE SHE WAS TELLING ME THE STORY of her life. I felt her pulse. It was normal. I pulled the covers up over her shoulders. Beside her pillow there was a notebook bound in cracked brown leather with an old brass lock. I pressed the little clip on the lock and the notebook snapped opened. Mrs Harrison had begun to tell me her story, so I saw no harm in reading about it myself. It turned out that the entries had been written long before the war by her mother in a beautiful old-fashioned Japanese hand. This is some of what it said …

Toshimitsu's elder brother has gone off to a place called 'Arkansas', but we decided to stay here in California. Our motivation is the same. Whoever harvests the first rice crop with success will call the other to him. I told Toshimitsu that I hoped his brother would fail, that California was far enough away from Japan for me, but he slapped me for my insolence, shouting in my face, 'Never say a word against my brother again!'

The heavy clay soils of the Sacramento Valley are not truly suitable for rice cultivation, but we persist, using the hardy Japanese variety Wataribune and sowing it with an ordinary grain drill. We try to convince other farmers in the area that California is the perfect place to grow rice. You can grow it in shallow soils that many farmers consider worthless.

Toshimitsu went to the capital, Sacramento, to meet the governor of California, to tell him of the great future his state would have if he encouraged Japanese people to come here and plant rice.

'Someday California will be sending the world's best rice to Japan, and Japan will be sending great steel weapons to America,' he said to the governor. This was not long after Japan's great victory in the war with Russia, and I think the governor believed him.

But the governor did nothing to help us. In fact, the farmers in our area were praying for us to fail. Letters with 'DEATH TO ALL ORIENTALS' were put in our letterbox, and one morning our only two horses were found dead in our stable. Toshimitsu called in the animal doctor to determine the cause of death, but the doctor officially recorded it as 'Unknown Disease, Death from Indeterminate Cause'.

'I didn't know that poison caused an unknown disease,' said Toshimitsu to the doctor, who merely shrugged his shoulders and left without saying another word.

I was hoping every night that we would succeed. I did not want to have to move to Arkansas, for one thing. For another, I wanted our little baby girl, Haruko, born on December 1, 1912, to grow up healthy and strong. If Toshimitsu failed, we might have to return to Kameoka, where my father had a small lumber business bringing logs down river from the mountains of Tamba and my father would …

I looked up at Haruko Harrison, trying to imagine her as a little girl running along an old fence on a farm in northern California so many years ago. Her face was that of many old Japanese women whom I had nursed in Tokyo before coming to Los Angeles, yet she had been born in America and had not once in her life set foot on Japanese soil. I returned to her mother's notebook, turning to the back of it …

SACHIKO THE NURSE READS THE DIARY OF HARUKO HARRISON'S MOTHER

Toshimitsu is back from his second trip to Japan since we emigrated. He sold the last of our family treasures in Japan in order to finance expansion of the farm, which we have been running now for well over twenty years. It is hard to believe that Toshimitsu's brother has been dead for over ten years now. I have long lost contact with his wife, Emiko, who took their three children back with her from Arkansas to live with her parents in Hiroshima.

At least we are able to make a living these days, though the people in northern California dislike Japanese now even more than before. 'You're the same as Indians,' said one man, a nearby landowner, 'except that they're red and you're yella. Succotash Americans, that's what I call every last goddamn one of ya.'

When Toshimitsu was told this he picked up a pitchfork, hopped into his truck and started to drive in the direction of the landowner's house. But when Haruko stood in front of the truck with her arms folded, he stopped, got out of the truck and, tossing the pitchfork into the dirt, stomped off. I'm glad that it was Haruko who was standing in front of the truck. If it had been me there, Toshimitsu probably would have tried to run me down.

Once in a while we would see a young tall fair-haired man standing like a statue on the edge of our property. I was bringing home some groceries with Haruko and I caught sight of him enveloped in dust churned up by the tyres. He was gazing in our direction with one hand shielding his eyes from the sun. I ordered Haruko into the house. She stared back at the man as she walked towards the house.

'If your father saw the look in your eye,' I told her, 'he'd put his pitchfork through you and the young man at the same time. You'd be skewered together, I tell you.'

Then there was a knock on our front door, and the man, introducing himself as George Bilson, said that he wanted to help us in any way we saw fit. Toshimitsu refused, telling him that Japanese people didn't need help to grow rice.

'I want to learn from you,' he said.

We allowed him to live in a little shed that Toshimitsu had built beside the stable. He worked very hard and never spoke to us unless asked something … just like a Japanese.

Except that he wasn't a Japanese. One night he went into town, coming back with a broken wrist and two eyes that stuck out like ripe dark plums.

'I got beaten up,' he said.

'Why?'

'For being a Jap lover.'

'Then don't be a Jap lover!' hollered Toshimitsu. 'Get away from us. We are like poison, don't you know? We poison the land with our filthy rice, we poison our horses just by being here, and we'll poison your skin until it turns yellow like ours!'

It was a lucky thing that Toshimitsu was speaking in Japanese, for George didn't understand a word.

'Thank you for getting angry in my behalf, Mr Yokoyama, sir,' he said, shaking Toshimitsu's hand vigourously.

Toshimitsu was embarrassed. He could only stand there having his hand shaken up and down by this tall blonde American man. Haruko laughed so hard … I—

'What? What happened?' said Mrs Harrison, squinting at me. (I immediately shut her mother's notebook and slipped it under her blanket.) 'Wait. Where am I?'

HARUKO HARRISON

I WOKE OUT OF THE DEEPEST SLEEP. THE NURSE WAS SITTING BY MY bed. I had been dreaming of the time when George came back from town with two enormous black eyes. Father felt sorry for him, but shouted at him nevertheless. Father's only way of showing sympathy for people was to shout at them a bit more softly than he did when he was cross with them.

I touched my mother's notebook below the blanket, gripped it and placed it on my chest.

'I was reading it,' said the nurse. 'I'm sorry.'

I told her that I was happy to have her read it, that I was once able to decipher the meaning of the Japanese words myself, but could do so no longer.

'Please take it, as a memento. My sons are not interested in their Japanese past. They would just throw it out. What did you say your name was again?'

'Sachiko.'

'Yes, that's right, Sachiko. I can't remember anything anymore except for what took place ages ago.'

We smiled at each other for a long time.

'Do you mind if I ask you something?' she said.

'Of course not.'

'What happened to George Bilson? Did you marry him?'

I started to laugh.

'Oh, forgive me. Did I ask something too personal?'

I assured her that I was not offended.

'George Bilson? George Bilson. I had forgotten his last name. I should have married him, yes. We ran away one night.'

'Perhaps I shouldn't be hearing this,' she said.

'No. It's all so long ago now. My parents are long gone, so it makes no difference to anyone.'

I told her what happened the night I eloped with George …

George had been convinced that rice would be the greatest crop on California's farms. Everybody was planting avocados and almonds and walnuts and olives, I mean. We had horrible telephone calls in the middle of the night with no one on the other end of the line, and this was in the days when a caller had to go through the operator to get through, so everyone in the town would have known who was making those calls. The windows and windshield on Father's truck were smashed, and once a delegation of farmers from around Sacramento came to us, offering help in planting other crops. But Father would not be moved. His dream was to sell California rice to Japan and Manshukoku … that was a new colony that Japanese people had set up in northern China.

One day George, who by then was eating dinner with us every night, asked my father and mother if he could marry me. Mother turned to Father, and Father refused outright, saying that I was not ready to be married and when I was they would send me back to Japan and arrange a marriage for me there.

'But Haruko is twenty-four years old,' said George.

'She has not reached her *konki*,' shouted Father.

'What is kon-key?' George asked me later that evening.

'Marriageable age.'

George went back to his shed without saying goodnight to any of us.

After Father and Mother went to sleep, I visited George in the shed. He was sitting at the table listening to the radio. A kerosene lamp was illuminating his face, making angular shadows that danced across it. I told him that I was of marriageable age and that I wanted to marry him. Believe it or not, two hours later we were on the road to Sacramento in George's Dodge, with our two small valises in the back seat.

The rest is somewhat blurred in my mind, Sachiko, but surely you are bored. What, go on? Oh, thank you. You are very kind …

The next thing I knew it was the middle of the night and I heard a loud banging on my hotel room door. I bolted up out of bed and asked who it was. It was Father, yelling at the top of his lungs. I opened the door, but he just continued to yell and holler so loud and fast that I couldn't understand what he was saying. He was angrier than I had ever seen him in my life. He held his pitchfork over his shoulder and dragged me in my pyjamas to the door of George's room.

Father banged on the door with the handle of his pitchfork, and when George opened the door a crack, Father forced his leg in, grabbed George by the scruff of his neck and pulled him out into the corridor. Father's anger had given him the strength of Shoki the Devil Queller, though Father did not have a beard like Shoki.

George was entirely naked. He was cupping his hands over himself. I didn't know whether I should cover my eyes or not. I was convinced that Father was going to ram the pitchfork into George's arched back.

Father put the pitchfork against George's buttocks. This caused George to stand up straight, this time without covering himself. Some of the other guests in the hotel had come out to see what the commotion was all about, but Father shouted at them in Japanese. Terrified, they all turned about and rushed into their rooms, slamming their doors shut.

Father forced George, without a stitch of clothes on, out of the hotel and onto the street. He made George walk down the middle of the street in the direction of the state capital building. All the while, I followed behind Father begging him to let George go. But all Father said was '*Omae wa damattero!*' (You shut up!)

When we reached the capital building, Father jumped up to the very top step. He held the pitchfork with both hands in the air, waving it about as if it was a halberd, chanting something in what sounded like ancient Japanese that I had never heard before and didn't understand. Then, after some minutes he fell to his knees, laid the pitchfork beside him and said, over and over again, in a normal voice, 'Rice rice rice rice rice rice rice rice …' The sun was just coming up, yet there wasn't a soul in sight, and … and …

I asked the kind nurse for a glass of water. I had forgotten her name again.

SACHIKO FINISHES THE STORY

I GAVE MRS HARRISON A GLASS OF WATER. SHE APPEARED TO HAVE lost her voice. I should not have let her talk on and on like that. She was such an old and frail woman. She gestured to me to open her mother's notebook and read the last page out loud. She stared at me the whole time as I read, tears streaming down her cheeks, as if she could hear her mother's own voice in mine …

I have been looking after Toshimitsu for eighteen months now. He has not recovered his speech, and hasn't been able to walk since the stroke. He spends half his days in bed, the other half in his wheelchair. The doctor, who has given him many pills, tells us that he could have another stroke at any time and that he must not be allowed to lose his temper over anything. This must be the bitterest pill for Toshimitsu to swallow. Oh, how he so loved to yell and scream at anybody and anything! He once shouted so loud at the neighbour's dog, an old cocker spaniel named Rusty, that the dog laid down on the grass patch in front of our house and died.

… Toshimitsu is dead. I telephoned Haruko in Los Angeles, where she is living with her husband, Jim, and she took the first train north for the funeral.

We buried Toshimitsu in Sacramento, and believe it or not, hundreds of people from farms as far away as two hundred miles came to see him off. A band from the local high school played 'Sakura, Sakura', and I held hands with Haruko, who was pregnant with her first child.

We both noticed him at the same time. It was George Bilson, standing at the back of the crowd. He had lost some of his bushy blonde hair … and sitting on his shoulders was a little girl … she couldn't have been much older than two. Haruko let go of my hand and bowed her head to him, then stared into the hole in the ground as her father's coffin was lowered into it.

Haruko left this morning. Back to Los Angeles. I returned to the farm by myself. The new owners, an American family named Bell, are allowing me to stay in the shed until my ship leaves San Francisco for Japan. Some people say that a war will break out between Japan and America, but I don't think it will, because Toshimitsu often said to me, years ago, that Japan and America are natural friends. 'You know why? We both have rice, that's why. Rice will always be the link between our two countries.' It was one of the only times in our life together that I had actually heard Toshimitsu whisper.

December 1940. I arrive in Kameoka. The rice crop in Japan is good. The rice crop in America is good….

I gave the notebook back to Mrs Harrison. With arms crossed, she clutched it to her chest.

'Thank you so much for reading my mother's words for me,' she said, smiling and letting the tears roll down her cheeks.

That had been the last entry in Mrs Yokoyama's notebook … *The rice crop in America is good….*

Some weeks later, Haruko Harrison passed away in the old people's home. Her sons were contacted, and I think that one of them came to take her body away. I'm not sure which son it was, because I wasn't on duty that day. The old Japanese notebook, with its cracked leather cover, had been left on her bedside table, along with a stack of birthday cards.

The Art of Saito Makoto

Please allow me to tell you about my husband, Saito Makoto.

I hope that you will not think me lacking in devotion for him when you hear his story. It is only now, many years after his death, that I am finally able to understand what happened to him myself.

Saito—I shall call him by his surname, as women of my generation were wont to do for their husbands—was a most talented painter, a man recognised at any early age for his gifts. The famous art critic, Masami Goichi, wrote of Saito …

His gift is undeniable. He reminds one immediately of Braque, but there are also undertones of playfulness, in the mood of Miro, Kandinsky and, if I may be so bold, Klee.

If there is a problem, however, it is this: Who is Saito? He is an artist who will have to find himself before he searches for anything else.

Masami Goichi wrote this in an issue of 'Geijutsu Shincho', Japan's leading postwar art magazine. Upon reading it, Saito ripped all of his copies, including the very first issue from 1950, to shreds. He did this with such force that it left him with a broken pinkie.

'I know bloody well who I am,' he hollered, throwing the shreds of multi-coloured magazine paper, like confetti, out our second-storey window. 'But I refuse to stand still, to run in place like other Japanese artists until they drop dead from exhaustion. I am going to reinvent myself. I am going to begin all over again. I am going to be reborn. Let Masami, who talks but never creates, go to hell, where he will no doubt find *himself!*'

I had never seen Saito so cross before. He was determined, from that time on, to make a name for himself in the Japanese art world. The best way in that day to do this was to go overseas, establish yourself in Europe or the United States and come back in triumph, famous.

We were living then at Futako Tamagawa, an outer suburb of Tokyo. Saito used to take long walks along the river, not coming back until dark. He would eat and drink, then set out to work throughout the night. I myself was working as a nursery school teacher in Seijo Gakuenmae. Saito was not selling many of his paintings, but we were not short of money by any means.

My father possessed considerable wealth, which he was able to hold onto despite the war. My father's father had built a successful business manufacturing bicycle frames. Everyone after the war wanted to own a bicycle, and the business went from strength to strength.

My family were very generous towards Saito and me. Father gave us the spacious flat that we were living in.

'Your husband is a man of genuine genius,' he told me. 'I am happy if I can help him express that genius, and so should you be.'

Father died in a bicycle accident in 1964, the year of the Tokyo Olympics.

Even though Saito had shredded all of his copies of 'Geijutsu Shincho', he was unable to rid Masami Goichi's words from his mind. Then, one day, he read some words written by the sculptor Alberto Giacometti, and those words changed his life … and mine.

The terrible thing is: The more one works on a picture, the more impossible it becomes to finish it.

Saito wrote a letter to Giacometti, telling him that this was 'a very Japanese concept', and that 'you have shown me a great truth about the artistic process, something that I had suspected but never grasped until today.'

Saito pored over Western art magazines, searching for photographs and prints of Giacometti's drawings and sculpture. On a very hot night around the time of the Obon Festival, he returned from one of his walks along the Tama River and went straight to his studio without eating or drinking. I heard him mumbling to himself in his studio and slid the door open. Saito was pacing the floor. I asked him what the matter was.

He stopped and looked at me sternly.

'The matter is that I have been trying to get too close to my subjects and have been losing myself in them. I require distance. I must meet Giacometti. I must!'

He started to pace the floor again, this time going around it, skirting the walls and bumping into the furniture. He refused all food for that day and the next, came down with a case of viral pneumonia and had to be hospitalised for ten days.

While Saito was in hospital, a registered letter arrived from Paris, and I rushed to deliver it to him. It was from Alberto Giacometti himself. He wrote ...

I am a great admirer of the Japanese and have a very good friend in Mr Isaku Yanaihara, the eminent professor and art historian.

If you wish to come to visit me, Mr Saito, I would be most pleased. My domicile is as written on the back of the envelope.

Upon reading this letter, Saito jumped up from bed, though he was still considerably feeble on his feet, and did his own variety of the Awa Odori dance around the ward. The other patients in the ward, mostly old men, sat up in bed and clapped their hands as Saito danced his way from one end of the corridor to the other.

When he returned home from hospital Saito was a new man. He started to create his art during the day as, apparently, did Giacometti.

'The light must be natural,' he said, gripping the paintbrush between his upper and lower front teeth. 'One must be absolutely objective. I have been dishonest in my art up to now, striving to live my life according to a pattern of what the modern Japanese artist deems "artistic". What a complete counterfeit I have been up till now!'

He carried his old paintings and drawings to the bank of the Tama River, going back and forth with bundles of them in his arms, and burnt every last one of them. Then he wrote an open letter to the editor of 'Geijutsu Shincho' proclaiming that his art had been false …

I renounce everything that I have done to date. The name Makoto Saito may be written at the bottom of those so-called artworks, but it is not the same Makoto Saito who is writing this letter. That counterfeit artist is dead. Long live the new Makoto Saito!

I was rather happy, actually, to see the new 'Makoto Saito'. As we were both now doing our work during the daytime hours, Saito and I were able to spend evenings together. Saito loved the theatre, taking me to see the latest plays by Kinoshita Junji and Tanaka Chikao, two leading playwrights of the day. He was even asked by Kinoshita Junji if he would create the set decoration for an upcoming production.

But Saito was unable to accept. He had made up his mind to go to Paris and meet the great master himself, Alberto Giacometti.

We had by then moved out of our flat in Futako Tamagawa. My younger sister, newly married and already pregnant, had taken it over. But father had bought us a large house, with ample room for Saito's studio, in Seijo 5-chome. This also brought me closer to the nursery school.

When I told Father that Saito wished to go to France to study art with a great master, he was overjoyed. He gave us three million yen, which was an enormous sum of money in those days.

'Tell Saito-san to take the money to Europe. It is a wonderful thing that he is doing. I suppose I wish that I could have become an artist, too. But people in Japan, both before and just after the war, needed bicycle frames more than picture frames. Now, with Japan recovered from the war, art and culture is what we need. Good luck to him.'

I went to Mitsukoshi Department Store on the Ginza and bought Saito the clothes he would need for Europe: six suits tailor made for him from English wool; neckties and ascot ties from England and France; American shoes; and a heavy Russian sable overcoat to get him through the winter.

I remember the day so vividly that I saw Saito off at the wharf in Yokohama. He stood high above me on the ship's deck, wrapped snugly in his shiny black overcoat. To either side of him were elderly Europeans or Americans … I cannot tell the difference. But no one was waving from the deck, not the elderly white people, and not Saito either.

*   *   *

I DID NOT SEE MY HUSBAND FOR MORE THAN TWO YEARS.

On the day of his return I put on my very best kimono, one handed down to me from my grandmother, charcoal grey with giant mauve chrysanthemums over its entire surface. Father insisted that I travel from Seijo to the wharf at Yokohama in his company limousine.

Saito had not written to me often; and though we had been married for three years prior to his departure, I somehow felt that I was travelling in that limousine to meet a half-stranger.

I waited outside the customs' area for several hours. It was a bitterly cold late December day, and I was happy that I had bought him the heavy fur coat. What Saito needed now was some good warm Japanese home cooking. I had awakened at the crack of dawn that day and prepared his favourite food for him, *nikujaga*, a hearty potato and beef stew.

I must admit to having suffered a shock that morning.

Emerging from the customs' area was my husband … but I cannot say that I immediately recognised him. He was gaunt nearly to the point of emaciation. His chin and cheeks were covered in a straggly greyish beard that resembled lichen on tree bark; and his skimpy clothes were, in a word, rags. He wore a red and white bandana around his neck and, on his head, an olive green beret with a hole in the side.

Saito was suffering from pleurisy. The driver of the limousine drove us from the wharf directly to the hospital; but Saito's pneumonia returned, and he passed away a week to the day after setting foot once again on Japanese soil.

What I came to realise, some time later, was that he had met Alberto Giacometti and believed that, to create art like his, he had to look like him and live his style of life.

The art critic Masami Goichi was wrong. Saito had not needed to find himself. He did know well who he was and where he came from. And he did find what he was looking for in Paris—true art. Sadly, he lost himself in the process.

When we scattered Saito's ashes onto the waters of the Tama River—which had been his last wish—I could not help but recall the shreds of the art magazines that he himself had flung out of our second-storey window with such conviction.

I am the last person to know whether or not his art will outlive him.

But I can still see him leaning out that open window overlooking the wide shallow river, speaking into the wind with a big smile on his face … 'I am going to begin all over again. I am going to be reborn.'

The Blue Angel

It was back in 1961 when it all came to an end. It isn't easy for me to recall things that happened so long ago. Not that much has taken place in my life since then. The past sixty years have been a bit of a blank. I sit here in my old age and observe my life across that blank without anger, but also without the fire of passion. It's as if my life went all cold after what happened.

I was singing in the lounge show at The Dunes in Las Vegas. The lounge was the space where musicians on the way up met those sliding down from dizzy stardom. It was an open area with large leather sofas, tables and chairs. You could order your drinks at the bar and have them taken to you by pretty blonde waitresses and tall handsome waiters. They had a baby grand there. One morning, way before any of the staff had come in, I saw Liberace practising on it. Though he was already famous by then, he enjoyed surprising guests wandering through there on their way to breakfast in the main dining room.

In the evenings we could hear the applause coming from the main dining room where the likes of Perry Como, Frank Sinatra and Dean Martin performed. Some of us timed our songs to end just when this applause came, to spill the sound of approval from 'the big place' onto us.

'Oh thank you, thank you, folks,' Max, our bandleader on piano, would say. 'Oh Lord, let some of that beautiful light shine down on us.'

I was singing in our black band. Max, as I said, was on piano; Bill on bass; Fred on drums; and Charlie on trumpet. Charlie was my boyfriend. He was the only member of the band who wasn't a person of colour. But he appeared under cork, though that practice had long gone out of fashion, and he had his hair blackened and curled like a Japanese yakuza gangster.

Once, just after a show, when all the guests had left the lounge for their rooms or the casino and Charlie was rubbing the black colour off his cheeks, the boys started ribbing him.

'Hey, man,' said Fred, 'will you look at that! Charlie's takin' his face off. Look at the phoney black man with the ivory cheeks. Looks like a goddamn piano keyboard.'

'Wish I could do that once in a while,' said Bill. 'Charlie's in two tone, like a spankin' new Cadillac. Shellac Cadillac.'

'It's like seein' a black-and-white movie in negative. Negative Charlie.'

Fred hit his drums, Bill plunked a few notes on his bass, and the two of them started improvising a song …

Negative man
Cadillac man
Who is your boss?
Who is your God?

Two-tone man
Where is you goin'?
And most of all …
Negative man
What is you doin' in a honky place like this?

Who is your boss
Negative man?
Who is your goddamn God?

At that Charlie walked off.

'Hey, where ya goin', man?' said Fred, walking towards him. 'Don't take no offense. If you think this is bad, you should see the sort of shit we get all the time.'

Charlie stopped on a dime. His face really did look like a keyboard.

'Now, you answer me,' continued Fred. 'Where was it you was from again?'

'Dublin, Republic of Ireland,' said Charlie softly.

'Republic of? Hey, did you hear that, boys? Tell us once more. I understood you, but I just likes the way you says it.'

'Republic of Ireland,' said Charlie, wiping his forehead and nose of the black colour with a handkerchief. 'You need me anymore?'

Charlie started to walk off again.

'Hey, wait up,' said Max, rising from his piano stool. 'We got some talking to do with you.'

'I'm tired and …'

'Shit, man, we're all tired. Angel here's tired.'

Max was now standing in front of Charlie.

'You're not on the move, that's your problem, little Charlie. Get me? You come all this way, to the edge of this godforsaken desert, just like that guy in the movie.'

'What guy?'

'You know, that guy in "Petrified Forest". What's his name? Howard. Leslie Howard, that's it. He comes all the way to the edge of the desert and then gets himself shot in the stomach by Duke Mantee.'

'Never heard of it. Never saw it.'

'Well, you should've seen it, Charlie. You should've. Duke Mantee, that's Humphrey Bogart, falls for the pretty girl there, that's Bette Davis. But she loves Howard 'cause he's a poet, like you, Charlie.'

'I'm not a poet. I'm nothing.'

'See, that's your problem, Charlie,' said Max, putting his hands on both of Charlie's shoulders. 'There's something eating you. You just not happy in your skin, man.'

'Eating me? Nothing's eating me.'

'Yes there is. You paint your face to be a black man like us, to blend into the music, as it were …'

'But you can't paint a heart … is that what you're going to say to me?'

Charlie grasped Max's forearms, as if to tell him to get his hands off of him.

'Hey, who said that, eh? Who in the hell said that, goddamit? Jesus Christ Almighty, you are one hell of a tightass Irishman, that's all I can say.'

Charlie walked off, but Max continued to talk to him in a voice that got louder and louder.

'Now, just go stomping off like that, fine. Leave when someone says somethin' you don't wanna here. Hey, hold up, Charlie. Hold up!'

Again Charlie stopped dead and turned around.

'Can I go now? This is a free country, isn't it?'

'Free country? Yeah, for some, I guess. Just answer one question we've all been wondering about.'

Charlie pulled a cigarette out of a packet of Luckies in his shirt pocket and lit it with a little silver lighter.

'We've all been wondering how you got to be called Charlie. Even Angel here. Even she doesn't know. Haven't you been wondering, honey?'

I nodded. I didn't know Charlie's full name either.

'He's named after Charlie Chaplin, I bet,' said Fred.

'Wait,' said Max. 'I got it. Charlie Parker. You took your name from Charlie-goddamn-Parker. See? He's not saying anything. Must be true. So, come on, Charlie, tell us what you were called when you were christened or whatever they do over there where you hail from?'

Charlie took a long drag on his cigarette.

'Rawdon Spoonthwaite. My father was a Protestant Irish …'

Max, Fred and Bill burst out laughing, but I didn't get what was so funny.

'Oooooeee,' said Bill. 'Rawdon Spooooon-thwaite. Oooee!'

Charlie flicked his cigarette onto a table and swivelled about.

'Now, don't go off on me again,' said Max. 'We're laughing because your name sounded like a Negro's, that's why. When it comes to handles, we've got the longest and fanciest on God's own Earth. Do you know how many little shiny black babies are Washingtons and Lincolns and Roosevelts? See Fred there? You know his real name? He's Roosevelt Woodrow Wilson Grover Cleveland … the Third! I mean, what's in a name anyway? It's just something your parents give you to make you into something they wanted to be themselves.'

'Can I go now?'

'Yeah, off you go, Charlie,' said Max. 'Off you go, man.'

I HAD KNOWN THAT CHARLIE WAS FROM IRELAND. HE HAD TOLD ME his life story up to then on our first date.

'I was one of eleven children,' he had said. 'One day somebody at home left the front door open and I walked out. I don't think anybody noticed, really. That's the lot.'

Not long after that Fred and Bill worked the lyrics they had sung to Charlie into a song. They called it 'Las Vegas Man' and it became my theme song in those lounge shows.

Las Vegas man
Who is your boss?
Who is your God?
Where have you come from?
And why are you here
Las Vegas man…?

There was nothing special about my own entrance into the desert. I grew up in Moji, a port town in northern Kyushu, in an ordinary Japanese family. My father was very strict. I was so afraid of him that I trembled whenever he spoke to me, which wasn't often. I had to write everything I wanted to say to him down beforehand and rehearse it, otherwise I would just freeze up like a trapped animal in front of him.

After the war I brought home an American sailor. Moji's port was occupied by the Marines. He wasn't a boyfriend or anything. He was just someone I had met on a street. My mother and father were appalled. Father beat me viciously that night for bringing home an American.

A month later I told them that I was leaving home to live with the guy, whose name was Walter Robinson. Mother went calmly into the next room and returned some minutes later. She had packed a small bag for me. She didn't say a word to me. She just handed the bag to me and walked out of the room. My father said only one thing to me.

'Never, never, whatever happens, come back here again.'

I obeyed him, as I had always done. After all, he was my father, and in those days a girl never disobeyed a father.

I lived with Walter until he was sent back home. It was just about the time that Japanese girls were allowed to marry American soldiers. We got married in a church in Moji. Of course, no one from my side of the family came to the church. Walter's family was in Los Angeles, so they couldn't come either. But about six of Walter's buddies from his squadron came, and my best friend, Hatsuko Kanemoto, was there too. Her parents had been forced to come to Japan from Korea before the war, but she thought of herself as a Japanese. I guess she was hoping to meet an American soldier too. She always told me, 'I don't dislike Japan. People keep to themselves. But I don't belong here. I want to go somewhere where I will belong.'

About half a year after arriving in Pasadena, California I left Walter. He used to call me his angel, then beat me black and blue. That's where I got my stage name from. And everybody said I always looked sad, so 'blue' suited me for that reason too.

I was pretty good at English and had a pleasant voice. Japanese girls were really popular in L.A. in the fifties. Umeki Miyoshi had taken the music world by storm and was singing at jazz clubs. A few years later she began appearing on TV and Broadway and in *Sayonara*, when she got an Oscar. She could even do a great *monomane*—sometimes Japanese words just come out and block the English word—I mean, impersonation, of Billy Eckstine.

I wouldn't have had a career at all if it hadn't been for a lucky meeting with Manny Lowe. His real name was Manny Lowenstein and he worked the nightclubs in downtown L.A. Manny suggested that I sing a song for one of his shows at the Oasis Club on South Western Ave. and 38th St. This was before the Oasis had become a club mainly for black performers. So I sang 'Come On-a My House', which I really loved. I adored Rosemary Clooney, who had made it a hit in America, and Chiemi Eri, who sang it in Japan. Chiemi Eri also sang 'Tennessee Waltz', which became one of my standards too.

Anyway, my version of 'Come On-a My House' that I sung half in English and half in Japanese, just like Chiemi Eri, was a big hit with the audiences at the Oasis. As I said, Japanese girls were really popular in L.A. then. I toured California with Manny, and he said that we should give Las Vegas a try. That was back in 1957.

'It's a clean place and lots of families go there,' he said. 'The dads are back from Korea and Japan and they'll really fall for you, Angel. Just keep speaking with that cute accent of yours and roll your eyes, you know, all coy and demure-like. They'll eat you up.'

We did a few tryouts at The Flamingo, The Desert Inn, where I saw Noel Coward walk across the lobby in a silk smoking jacket, and The Thunderbird. But it was The Dunes that took us on in their lounge. That's where I met Max. He was playing solo piano in the lounge at dinnertime, when people who couldn't afford to eat in the main dining room would order hamburgers and spaghetti and food like that and eat it there.

The trouble was, though, that the manager at The Dunes didn't like Manny's *shtick*, as he called it. He said that Manny's brand of humour wasn't healthy enough for Las Vegas, and Manny was fired.

'You stay on here, Angel, honey,' he said to me. 'Who knows, someday you may even be giving me an audition.'

I never saw Manny again after that.

IT WAS MAX WHO TOOK ME ON. MAX WAS THE MOST TALENTED musician I had ever met. He had trained as a classical pianist, and he could write songs, sing and do the most amazing impersonations. One night, after a few people who had been at the main show had trickled into the lounge and ordered drinks, Manny sat at the piano and started playing some classical music, I think it was Beethoven or something. The people were really impressed. Then he stood up and did an impersonation of a black Charles Laughton playing the hunchback of Notre Dame. Just when everybody was cracking up, he got down on his hands and knees and sang 'Mammy' in a voice that sounded just like Al Jolson's, but with a Jewish accent.

'Thanks, folks,' he said when the people there stood up and applauded him. 'That's my version of "My Yiddishe Mammy". I figure, if a Jew can do a Negro's song, a Negro can return the compliment.'

The manager who had fired Manny was a Ukrainian American named Ed. No one could pronounce his last name. He had been standing in the back of the lounge when Max was doing his impersonations.

'Someday, Max,' he said, coming up to him after the performance, 'you may be able to do that sort of thing in America, but not now, pal. You stick to what you're good at, pal, your own stuff. Don't cross the line, you hear? People don't come to Vegas to get insulted.'

I didn't understand what the manager meant when he said Max had insulted people. If he had, they sure loved being insulted.

It wasn't long before Fred, Bill and Charlie joined Max and they formed the band. That's when Charlie came into my life.

THE NIGHT THAT CHARLIE TOLD US HIS REAL NAME, I FOLLOWED him to his dressing room behind the main stage in the dining room. I knocked on the door.

'Yeah, who is it?'

'It's me, Charlie. Angel.'

He opened the door.

'Can I come in?'

He gestured for me to come in with a sweep of his arm, like one of the Three Musketeers would do for a lady. But I hadn't taken more than a step or two before he grabbed me from behind and turned me around, giving me big kisses on my cheeks, nose and mouth.

'Charlie, your face!'

'What's the matter with my face?' he asked, kissing me hard on the lips.

I pulled away from him as best as I could.

'Charlie, you've still got that black stuff on your chin. It'll get all over me.'

'So? You've still got your makeup on. I've got mine. We've got the same face now, Angel.'

He put his arms tightly around me and kissed me passionately. Then he stepped back and stared at my face.

'You look like an overripe banana,' he said.

WHEN I FIRST ARRIVED IN AMERICA WITH MY HUSBAND WALTER, who I never actually divorced, I was puzzled by something Americans said. They said that things were 'skin deep', like, especially beauty. I didn't know what that meant. All Charlie would tell me, when I asked him what 'skin deep' meant, was that my beauty went down all the way to my heart.

We made love in the dressing room that night. I was lying on the old couch that was there and Charlie was on top of me. A couple of the springs had come up right to below the surface of the upholstery, and I had to wiggle about a lot to get my bottom between them. It was lucky that my bottom was so narrow.

After we made love, I changed into a yukata that I kept in Charlie's dressing room and Charlie knelt at my feet. He took the hems of my yukata and pulled them apart. I quickly put my knees together.

'Charlie, stop it,' I said, folding the left hem of the yukata over the right.

'Okay,' he said, reaching across to the little pine table beside the couch and pulling a cigarette from the packet that was on it.

'Charlie, why did you come here in the first place?'

He lit the cigarette with his lighter and inhaled deeply.

'To Vegas?'

'To this country.'

'Hmm. Well, from where I come from everyone wants to go to America at least once. They want to try their luck inside a dream and maybe never have to wake up.'

'Did you want to be a star?'

'Me?'

He spit out a little shred of tobacco that had stuck to his tongue.

'Did you think you could make it here?' I asked him.

'Nope. Not me. I'm the sort of bloke who always stays in the background, the kind they say about, "No, I didn't see anyone standing back there? Was he a part of the band?" You're what they make stars out of, Angel. Someday Sinatra or Martin or someone like that will wander into the lounge and put their dibs on you.'

'Dibs?'

'Yeah. Mitts. They'll put their name on you, like a tattoo on your arm. Before you know it you'll be singing beside one of the stars in the dinner shows. A duet, you know, something like 'Baby It's Cold Outside'. You'll see your name up in the marquee in front of the hotel. Tonight, in the main dining room, the one, the only … Japanese Angel!'

'Just Angel, Charlie. I'm not a Japanese anymore when I'm here.'

'Okay. Angel. But as for me,' he said, stubbing out the cigarette in a thick chipped glass ashtray, 'I'm like that bloke in the movie, the bloke who comes to the desert to find himself and loses sight of everything in the end, including himself.'

I leaned over and kissed the back of his neck. I particularly like that part of Charlie's body. It had a smell like one I remember from the docks at Moji Port. He put his arms under me and laid me on my stomach on the couch. Then he lifted the yukata off my legs, spread my legs and straddled my body, putting his erect penis inside me with his right hand. I loved what he was doing; but one of the springs was poking right into the space between my breasts. It made it hard for me to concentrate.

Just then there was a knock on the door. This stopped Charlie from thrusting further into me, which is just as good because the spring was making a loud creaking noise that would have alerted anyone at the door to what we were doing.

'Angel, you in there?'

It was Ed, the manager. Charlie nodded to me as he stood up.

'Yes, Ed.'

Charlie pulled on his underwear, which wasn't easy because his penis was sticking right out the corner, like a carrot.

'Stop laughing at me,' he whispered, 'and go open the door.'

I rose from the couch, adjusted my yukata, went to the door and opened it.

'Sorry,' said Ed, entering. 'I hope I'm not interrupting …'

'No, you're not,' said Charlie, picking up the butt of the cigarette from the ashtray.

'How did you like the show, Ed?' I asked, walking to the back of the room and leaning against a row of costumes hanging in an open closet.

'Yeah, pretty good. Better than when that Jew-boy comedian was here. It was *schlocky* then. Isn't that what those people say?'

'I wouldn't know,' said Charlie.

'What we need is a Jerry Lewis or a Danny Kaye. They're Jews of a different colour. They don't push it in your face. They blend in, know what I mean? Anyhow, I came here to tell you both that I've been talking with Max and I told him I'm extending all your contracts for another six months. The lounge is popular with people. They like to see a little Jap girl like Angel. They feel kind of, you know, kind of like they want to protect you.'

'Protect me? From what?'

'I dunno. You know, your own people. I mean, the men there. A lot of the fellas who come here had buddies killed by your men. But they got nothing against you, Angel. Nothing at all. They know you didn't start any war. You get them all excited, know what I mean? All worked up. They can feel the red blood pumping inside them when they see you, Angel. And that's what Vegas's all about. It's about getting people excited so they can do whatever they want here. You can do whatever you want here. God made this little place in the desert so that people can be really free to be themselves.'

Ed walked out of the dressing room, shutting the door behind him. Charlie wanted to take up where we had left off, but I was tired. He asked me what he was supposed to do with his penis, which was just as long and hard as it was before, maybe that's why he had sat down on the couch and crossed his legs when Ed was there.

'Close your eyes and think of Japan,' I said, throwing him a kiss from the doorway.

FRED AND BILL USED TO GO INTO THE ALLEY BEHIND ONE OF THE wings of The Dunes, crouch between the trash cans and shoot up. I don't know how or when it happened, but they lured Charlie back there once and gave him his first fix. Charlie was doing it just for a lark, I guess. He wasn't depressed or bitter. He just felt insecure, to use his own word. When I asked him why he started doing it, all he said was, 'Couldn't find a good reason not to.'

If Max had found out he would've killed him. Max thought the world of Charlie. I think he saw Charlie as a kind of son. Maybe it was because Max had had a little brother named Charlie. When I asked him where his brother Charlie was, he said, 'Father took him.'

'I don't understand, Max.'

'Father, Angel. The Lord God.'

Fred told me that Max's little brother Charlie had overdosed on heroin.

Max, who had played with Louis Armstrong, always said that my Charlie could be a great horn player if he only applied himself.

'Get yo' big white ass over here,' he said to Charlie one night.

We had been rehearsing a new song in the lounge long after everybody had gone to sleep, except for a few of the staff at the bar who never paid much attention to us anyway.

'I is gonna teach you somethin', white boy, that you ain't nevah gonna learn at no Jooliahd!'

Max, who had graduated from the Juilliard School of Music, was impersonating the way of talking of Bert Williams, who he had seen live on stage when he was a boy. Charlie shuffled over to the piano.

'Good, now, don't be shy. Stand shoulder to shoulder with me. Oh my, you is tall, you is a tall white boy! Now, do a little soft shoe with me. C'mon, you can do it. Look, dudes, the ofay's not bad. I think whitey's got natural rhythm.'

Charlie, who was doing a slow tap, started dancing an Irish jig, circling Max as he went through the steps.

'Atta boy. That's good. Yes, you is loose where it counts, in the joints. Now slow down. Slower. Slower.'

Charlie was dancing around Max in slow motion. He was barely moving. Suddenly Max embraced him and the two stood like that in front of the piano.

'God gave you a big heart, Charlie, he did. That's so much more important than any talent. Look at us. We got a lot of talent. And where does it get us. Our talent is skin deep, as far as the audience is concerned. We're all losers in their eyes, Charlie, that's why they don't mind clapping for us. Except for you and Angel, Charlie. You two stick together. You got what America wants.'

Max dropped his arms. His eyes were welling with tears. It was then that Fred blurted it out.

'Hey, I thought we were gonna ease our pain tonight.'

Max jerked his head back and stared up at Charlie's face.

'Is he talking about what I think he is talking about?'

Charlie didn't answer. Max took two steps back and turned his gaze on us. He knew then that Charlie was shooting up in the back alley with Fred and Bill. He pursed his lips and nodded.

'Okay. Okay. It's your life. Maybe that's what the manager man meant by freedom. The freedom to … to … be your own man. That's America, man. That's really America, white and naked and dead all over.'

Max was getting all choked up. He turned and walked out of the lounge. Charlie sat down on the piano stool. Fred and Bill started putting away their instruments. I didn't know what to do. I was the last person to know what I was doing there.

In July 1961, on one of the hottest days on record in Nevada, a man and his wife came into The Dunes. He was an Episcopalian minister. Their Plymouth had broken down about eight miles out of town and they had to stay at the hotel until it could be fixed.

Las Vegas has quite an effect on most men, and I was used to them falling in love with me. Sitting in the lounge and listening to me sing to them … who knows, maybe they were recalling some sweetheart from the time they were in Japan just after the war. I remember how my sailor Walter had fallen for me. He had proposed marriage halfway through the first night we went on a date.

But Jonathan Drammen fell very hard. I guess he had never experienced any real kind of passion before. He came into the lounge every night, even though his wife Jenny was visibly disgusted by everything she saw in Las Vegas. She couldn't wait for the car to be fixed and for them to be out of there.

After about six days—the garage had to bring a part from L.A.—their car was ready to go, but Jonathan Drammen wasn't. He told his wife to go home without him. I heard them arguing with each other in the main lobby. She asked if he was suffering from some sort of heat stroke. 'The sun or something here has made you crazy,' she said. He said that he was as fine as he ever was and that he wanted to stay on 'for a spell'. 'A spell?' she said. 'How long is a spell?' He just shrugged his shoulders and turned away from her. Then he stopped, faced her again and said in a loud voice that echoed throughout the lobby, 'Sell the car in Denver and fly to your brother's place in Boston.' He turned about again and disappeared down a long corridor.

I hadn't encouraged any of this. Jonathan had come to my dressing room after a show. I had been expecting Charlie. Charlie and I often had a nightcap in my dressing room before going up to our room in the hotel. Jonathan fell to his knees. It looked like he was praying or something. He was staring at my legs, which I promptly covered up by closing my kimono over them.

Normally I would never have allowed any man to come into my dressing room. But I had left the door open for Charlie. Charlie and I had had a fight the night before about him being hooked on drugs. He stormed out of our room. I think he went to the back alley all by himself. I drank half a bottle of red wine before my head started spinning like a propeller and I fainted on the floor beside the bed.

All I had on in my dressing room was my loose silk kimono decorated with plum blossoms and sparrows, the only valuable piece of clothing I had taken with me from Japan. I was wearing no underclothes. When I stood up my kimono opened. Jonathan looked up. He could see my private parts and everything. I swiftly covered myself up, but Jonathan crawled to my feet and started kissing them. I jumped backwards to get away from him. I knew that he would never hurt me, but I couldn't let any man do that to me. I have never seen a man so overcome by passion as he was. His whole body was shaking and he kept opening and closing his mouth as if gasping for air. He held his fingers open, raised into the air as if pointing to Heaven.

'I'm sorry, I'm sorry,' he kept saying. 'I don't know what has come over me. I'm sorry. Please forgive me.'

The door swung open. I was actually hoping that Charlie would find me like that. Nothing ever got Charlie upset. Maybe Charlie would feel a little jealous now.

But it was the manager Ed who came in. Jonathan stood up immediately, brushing himself off. He tried to straighten out his Roman collar, but he just kept pushing it from one side to the other. He stared at me without saying a word and took some steps backwards, knocking the nape of his neck against the brass hook on the inside of my door.

'It's nothing,' he said, swinging the door wide open. 'I'm not myself.'

Jonathan turned about and left.

'I just came to see if you were all right, Angel,' said Ed.

'I'm fine. I need some time to change.'

Ed nodded and walked out, quietly shutting the door.

Charlie didn't come to my dressing room that night. In fact, he didn't get back to our room until the early hours of the morning. He was stoned.

'Charlie, where have you been?' I asked.

'Oh, around. I was with Brill and Fed … I mean, Bill and Fred.'

He whirled around and fell backwards onto the bed.

'Charlie!'

'I'm fine, Angel. Never felt better in me life.'

He sat up and took my hand in his.

'I had this amazing vision, Angel.'

'Vision?'

'Yeah. The president went up to Heaven and he gets to God who's sitting in front of this enormous television set eating a TV dinner. "Hey, Jack," says God, "remind me to rethink frozen peas when I get a moment. You know, I wasn't expecting you so soon." So Kennedy says, "Geez, God, first I want to thank you for making me the second most powerful man on Earth, after your own son, that is. And secondly, I want to thank you for making me a Catholic." So God looks up from his TV dinner, puts down his plastic knife and fork and says, "What in the fuck is a Catholic?"'

At that Charlie burst into such uncontrollable laughter that he started coughing and choking. I had to lay him on the bed and stroke his chest to get him to stop.

'Let go of me,' he said.

'What? Charlie, it's me. You're stoned, you ...'

'I said get your hands off me.'

I pulled away from him but remained like that on the bed. Suddenly he was scowling at me like one of those angry gods guarding the gateways to Japanese temples. My leg was touching his. I gently rubbed his knee and said '*Anata*' (Darling) in Japanese.

'This place is a void,' he said, 'a total void. It's more empty than any place in the world. If you get sucked into here, you don't get out. This place devours you. I'm nothing. I'm nothing anywhere. But I'm even less than nothing here. I've ceased to exist for anybody. For you too.'

'You do exist for me, Charlie. I love you. I really do. If we can leave here I want to have your baby. We can leave and ...'

'Baby? Yeah, fancy me a father. Any child of mine would be totally disadvantaged. Scarred for life. I'd make an even worse father than my own, and, believe me, he was pretty bloody bad. The boys in the band are okay. They fit the bill for all the rich white bastards who come here. Oh, those people love their Negroes. Play it again, Sam. Give us that old black Joe routine, that ...'

'Charlie, shut up! Just shut up!'

'No, you shut up.'

'Charlie, why are you doing this to me? It's the drugs. They've made you into something you aren't.'

'You call yourself a blue angel, eh?' he said, grabbing me by the wrist and wrenching my hand away from him. 'Well, okay, you are an angel. I'll grant you that. But you're a yellow angel, that's what you are. So get the fuck out of my life, yellow angel!'

Charlie stood up with difficulty, tucked his shirt into his trousers and walked out of the room. I burst into tears and covered my face.

To this day I don't know what came over Charlie. I guess he had come to the edge of the desert—no, right into the middle of the desert—lost his way and couldn't find himself.

Max replaced Charlie with another trumpet player, who was a real black. Jonathan Drammen wrote me a note, saying how sorry he was for 'forgetting myself'. He had left the next morning by bus for Denver, where his wife Jenny was apparently waiting for him. Ed, the manager, said that he heard the story of a respectable German professor in Germany before the war. The professor had fallen for a cabaret singer and had 'totally degraded his life', as Ed put it. 'At least your man of God got out of here while the getting was good. There are some people who can pull themselves out of Hell. And there are those who never do.'

I stayed on at The Dunes until the fall of that year, 1961. Max had written a new song for me called 'My Dream', about a place where dreams are colour blind and where nobody has to put on a face that isn't his own. But people didn't want to hear that song in America at that time. They kept asking for their favourite, 'Las Vegas Man'.

When I left Las Vegas, Ed gave me a really sweet gift. It was a little silver charm of a *torii*, the tall gateway to a shrine in Japan. He said he had bought it for his wife when he was stationed in Tokyo after the war, but that she died the year after he returned to Chicago. 'That's when I moved out here, to the desert. We had no children,' he said, 'so

I have no one to give it to except you, Angel.'

'Thank you, Ed,' I said, giving him a kiss on the cheek.

He blushed and touched his cheek.

'Does it remind you of your home in Japan?' he asked.

'Yes, it does.'

After that I returned to Los Angeles. I thought of getting in touch with Walter so that we could get legally divorced. But I didn't really want to see him again. I've managed to look after myself by teaching Japanese to Nisei and Sansei Japanese Americans who want to find out something about their ancestral home by speaking with the older generation of Japanese immigrants in Los Angeles. As for me, I haven't made an attempt to contact my parents. I have taken them at their word never to go back home.

No one knew where Charlie went after Las Vegas. He would never have gone back to Ireland, I know that. There was really nowhere for him to go where he could find himself. I guess he had given up on himself.

But at least he had managed to pull himself out of a place that was at least as hot as Hell.

That's one thing that Charlie and I definitely had in common. We knew where we didn't belong.

The Life and Times

The pit in my stomach was open for all to see.

All I was capable of doing was lying stiffly on my back, a virtual corpse, with my neck angled upwards in front of me, peering into it, my neck the stalk of a white lily, my head the flower. I felt that if I dared to move, I would be swallowed up into that pit and be lost in it. Ah, this would make an amusing, if grotesque, portrait by an Edo-period artist: *Girl Swallowed up in the Pit of her Stomach.*

How can I be staring into myself like this, bereft and yet totally aware? Why is there no pain at all, just a dull sensation, a numbing all over, as if time has come to a standstill and I am just an observer, a visitor at a museum transfixed by a painting of myself?

The next night it was the same, only now the pit was wider, filling up gradually with a cloudy liquid as if from a little tube leading to it from somewhere else in my body … my spleen? … my brain? … my heart? My genitals? Once again I gazed deep inside myself with my head propped up like a little wooden puppet's head on a stick, everything else still yet uncontrollable.

The next thing I knew, as I strained my eyes to look into the liquid with its mawkish smell, I could see tiny snakes, pale green, swimming about with full freedom just below the surface, slithering in one direction and then another, gliding along the sides of the pit as if they were having the time of their life.

This terrified me, and I clamped my eyes shut to make the uncanny and ugly vision disappear. When I opened my eyes and dared to look down again, not only were the pool and the liquid and the snakes gone, but the pit itself had vanished, and the white skin of my belly was as flat smooth and seamless as ever.

'Ah,' I whispered to myself, sitting up in bed and adjusting my two pillows to support my neck, 'that liquid in your stomach was poison, the muck of your own ego, Abby, dripping inside you. And the snakes were there to frighten you away from your ego. They were by-products of its fantasies. No … ridiculous. No meaning at all. Just a bloody garden-variety nightmare.'

I twisted my body around in bed and placed both feet firmly on the floor, throwing the sheet off my calves. The yellow numerals on the digital clock read 3:56.

'Shit,' I thought. 'I didn't fall asleep till after midnight. The last time I looked at the clock it read 12:14.'

I hadn't even slept four hours. I was in the habit, since childhood, of noting, as best as I could, the last moment before falling asleep and then glancing at the clock the instant I awoke. I put my palm over my stomach as if to assure myself that the open pit that I had seen in such clear detail was covered by skin. I rubbed the skin between my navel and my pubic hair. I let my hand slip down to my vagina and started to gently stroke my clitoris with the middle finger of my left hand.

'Nope, no good,' I said to myself in an unexpectedly loud voice. 'The little snakes flitting around ruined the mood. See, Dr Freud? Your Western analyses don't work here in Japan. Maybe later after a cup of coffee I'll try again. Maybe after I get that goddamn article written. Maybe I'll be able to bring myself a bit of pleasure then.'

I reached out to the bedside lamp and, putting my hand below the shade, pulled on the little chain. The yellow angle of light threw crisscrossing shadows of my breasts onto my belly. I looked at myself in the long mirror on the wall opposite me. I reached out again, this time for the glass of soda water that I had left undrunk on the bedside table.

'Abby Eisenglass,' I thought, 'you will put an end to these stupid nightmares. You've seen too much Japanese art, that's your problem. You have got a story to write and, thank goodness, it is *not* the story of your own life. There is no better way of getting out of yourself than by plunging yourself into the story of someone else's life, particularly a story from a different time than your own.'

I stood up and wriggled out of my pyjama bottoms. The elastic at the top had become so loose that they fell easily to my feet. I stared at myself in the mirror—full frontal. I admired myself for a few moments. Why not? A woman of twenty-eight, in good health, living away from her country in Tokyo, living as free as a bird … why not take yourself in, Abby, and love what you see? If you don't love yourself, what man ever will?

I had been to Kobe to interview Maria Emilovna Teploukhova for the Culture Day issue of the English-language daily that I worked for. Mr Murota, my editor, had given me strict instructions.

'I am not interested in the stale memories of an old woman, Abby-san. I want you to come back to Tokyo with a portrait of Japan as it was in the old days, when this lady was your age now. It's only by such comparisons that our Japanese readers can see how Japan has changed. Otherwise, they tend to think it's been essentially the same, as far as relationships go, since Meiji.'

I threw on a tie-dyed yukata that I had bought in Narumi near Nagoya when I went there to do a story on traditional fabric design. I left the front of it open as I walked through the dark corridor of my flat into the kitchen. A grey light filtered through the cheap curtains. I opened the refrigerator, squinting at the bright light, and thrust my hand behind several jam jars to the knob that adjusted the brightness, turning it down to a dim glow.

'What are you doing in the kitchen?' I said to myself out loud. 'It's not even four in the fucking morning. Go back to bed. Okay, will do. Good girl. Thank you. I am a good girl.'

I often held conversations with myself like this. It made me feel that I wasn't living alone. And it was more of a lively exchange of words than I had ever conducted with Greg. Greg was the silent type. In fact, he never said a fucking word. One day he turned to me in bed and said, 'I have something to tell you.'

'That's unusual,' I said, turning towards him and resting my head on my palm.

'I'm leaving.'

'Okay.'

'Are you okay with it?'

'Yeah, if you're okay.'

'Yeah, I'm okay,' he said, pecking me on the forehead.

'Where're you off to?'

'Me? I'm going home. Back to Leeds. I've had enough of Japan. It's too hard to make friends here.'

'Well, maybe if you said a few words to people they would say something back.'

'It's not that. Japanese people are silent types just like me. But you can't read these people. They keep everything to themselves. That's why I loved you, Abby. You always wear your heart on your sleeve.'

'Do I?'

'You do. It's sweet. But I've gotta go. Dad's getting me a job at one of his pubs. He says a lot of Japanese come there, so I can practise my Japanese all I want.'

The next day Greg was gone. I can't say that I've missed him either. There wasn't much passion between us. Oh, there was sex, a lot of it. But it wasn't the kind of great sex you'd write home about. Just sort of, um, mechanical. Perfunctory, that's the word. I mean, Greg made all the right motions, but screwing him was like screwing a robot with software from about 2002. Once he came, he'd stretch out as if loosening the nuts in his joints, assume a prone position on the bed and close his eyes. It was as if someone had turned off a switch in him and put him into sleep mode.

It was 4:07 when I got under the covers again. Then it was 4:12 … 4:21 … 04:40. 'No use in trying to fall asleep again,' I told myself. 'Get yourself going, girl, and do the job.'

I bolted out of bed, raised both hands so high that I felt I could touch the ceiling, tossed aside the yukata and dressed in the clothes I had draped over my desk the night before: pink undies and white sports bra, jeans and a kaftan I had picked up in a preloved clothing shop in Harajuku. I switched on my computer and sat down in front of it, waiting for the monitor to light up with a screensaver that I had created myself, a picture of Hokusai's great wave about to crash down on top of the White House with the president and other world leaders entering a submarine on the roof, preparing their 'getaway'. I lifted the cup of coffee that I had left the night before beside my keyboard and took a sip. It tasted surprisingly good.

'The fate of a woman is decided more by her times than by the company she keeps,' I wrote on the document I had titled 'The Life and Times of an Émigré in Japan'.

I slowly raised my hands off the keyboard. I took another sip of cold coffee and rubbed a little smudge of chocolate off the computer screen with my forefinger, only managing to spread it over a larger area.

'No. Awful,' I whispered to myself, deleting this first line of my article on Maria Emilovna Teploukhova. 'It's a good job I didn't end up like her. I'm not going to spend my whole life in this country. No way.'

I surprised myself. First of all, why, I wondered, should I ever compare myself with a lady who is a hundred and two years old from a country like Russia? Second, I had picked up a few British expressions from Greg, like 'it's a good job' and 'too clever by half'. I even called our apartment a 'flat'. I guess it's the only thing I took out of the relationship, a few expressions and a half-finished short story I was writing called 'I Slept with a Robot'. We haven't even exchanged emails since he arrived home, Greg and I. Not so much as a skype. We had nothing more to say to each other. I mean, how do you commiserate with a slab of metal? It was like having a love affair with the Tin Man in 'The Wizard of Oz' before Dorothy squeezed oil into its joints.

No, Maria had been left in life with no money, no career and no love from the man she worshipped and adored. That wasn't going to happen to me. How could it? I had money, well, a bit, and a budding career in journalism ... and if there wasn't any love in my life at present, who knows what's not waiting for me just around the corner? I flashed to the picture of my naked self in front of the mirror. Some man was going to get all that and more. It had to be only a matter of time before he turned the corner and bumped into me, crisscrossing shadows, loose elastic and all.

I leaned back in my swivel chair and peered up at the ceiling. Memories of times with Hideaki flashed through my mind. I had met him in San Diego, where he had gone to do a PhD on the free-living nematodes of Coronado Island. Unfortunately he spent more time under the lights at the casino in the Hotel del Coronado than in the brackish waters of the island where his worms were wriggling about. I had gone down to the island with a girlfriend to do some snorkelling. We caught sight of him on the beach at the same time and both instantly fell for him. Luckily I was the one who spoke some Japanese, thanks to doing a waitressing job at an okonomiyaki restaurant in L.A.'s Little Tokyo.

That night Hideaki and I made passionate love. God he was good! His body was so elastic, it was as if two or three men were slithering over my every nook and cranny at the same time. Talk about snakes! But Hideaki lost a lot of money playing Black Jack and decided to 'hightail it home', to use his own words. His English was so good that he got a high-paying job at a *juku*, a cram school, in Ebisu, a trendy suburb of Tokyo. He sent me an air ticket and, before I knew it, I was living with him at his gorgeous apartment in Meguro.

But the difference between me and Maria is that I made the decision to leave Hideaki, while she was tossed aside by her man like a strip of old cloth. It was true that Hideaki was good in bed. But he was good not only in my bed but in the beds of lots of other girls. So I picked myself up, dusted off my laptop and offered my services to Japan's leading English-language daily newspaper. And I was hired on the spot! Yes, a girl can take her fate into her own hands. Maybe Maria should have realised that once upon a time.

'The era may be distant from us in today's bustling Japanese metropolises, but the message is the same: A woman must take her life into her own hands.'

That was the new opening sentence of my in-depth article on the life and times of Maria Emilovna Teploukhova. I craned my neck and turned about to check the time on my digital clock. It read 5:42. I lifted the cup to my lips and drained it of coffee. There was a sludge of grains at the bottom. I rubbed the tip of my tongue over both the top and bottom rows of my teeth, dislodging the sludge and drooling it out of my mouth back into the cup.

'No,' I thought. 'This won't do either.' I deleted the sentence that I had just written. It was nearing 6:00 and I hadn't been able to write a single line.

'What is the matter with you, Abby Eisenglass?' I said to myself aloud, standing up and throwing myself onto my bed. 'Why are you having such trouble getting into this story? It should be a piece of cake. Just write up what the old lady told you in Kobe. Let her speak for herself. That's how the best stories get written, isn't it? They write themselves. Pretend she's like a wizened old Holden Caulfield. Let her open herself up to the readers on her own terms. You should not be visible between her and the readers.'

I had it now. I wasn't really necessary. I mean, I was only going to be the medium. Her own words would reach readers directly once they had passed seamlessly through me. They had to be unchanged, *sonomama*, just 'as is'. She had to appear to readers as if she was standing in front of them, talking personally to each and every one of them. I wasn't in the equation. But how do you take yourself out of the equation? I still had to work that out.

It was 8:41. I was back at my desk but had not managed to commit so much as the first sentence to my article. I kept reviewing the facts in my mind. Maybe the facts would kick start a reaction so that I would race along.

Maria Emilovna Teploukhova had arrived in Kobe via Shanghai from Harbin in 1937 with her husband, Konrad.

'Konrad was a brilliant linguist,' she had told me. 'He spoke fluent Russian, of course English, also French, German and Chinese. He mastered Japanese in a matter of weeks and became the first Russian to translate the poetry of Kenji Miyazawa into his native language. He even received a personal letter from Maksim Gorky praising his translations and was overjoyed, until he realised that Maksim Gorky had died in 1936 and the letter must have been written by someone else, maybe someone in the NKVD who was luring him back to the U.S.S.R.

'Oh yes, Konrad was an émigré, like me, what you would call today an "expatriate". But it's wrong to think that all people who leave their country hate it. He was Russian through and through, and he wasn't even anti-communist. Many of the Russians who left were sympathetic to what was happening in the Soviet Union at the time, yet simply found it too difficult personally to fit in there, do you know what I mean? It was easier being an armchair communist. You could talk about some of the good things in your country without having to be there. Distance makes the heart more patriotic, or at least it does in some people.

'And since you were a foreigner here in Japan, you just floated above everything and everyone. People looked up to you. You were detached. You felt a lot of freedom that way, a freedom you don't have in your own country, even in America or Europe. I suppose it's really the same now. In a foreign country you only have to commit your intellect. You don't have to commit your blood like you do in your own country, be it Russia then or America or anywhere else now. I said "armchair communist", but what I meant was "easychair communist". That's what we all were ... until the war started, that is. Then we all had to get out of our chair, stand up and be counted as one thing or another.

'Things really changed around 1939. Konrad, whose real last name was Ostrov, started to use a new last name as a nom de plume. It was Teploukhov. That's the name I still use now. Do you know what it means in Russian? No, how could you? It means "warm ear". That's me, Mrs Warmear. Sounds nice, no? But even as Stalin was torturing and murdering more and more innocent people, Konrad still cherished the ideals of the Soviet Union at its founding. Not being there he didn't have to dirty his hands. Float, float, dear émigré, float over the pools of blood below you! Sorry, we Russians love our poetry. Oh, it's only something I wrote. I've never published my poetry. It's only for me to read.

'As you can imagine, Abby, life for Konrad became increasingly difficult during the 1940s. For some reason we weren't thrown into jail. We moved to the countryside into a little cottage on the outskirts of Hanamaki, the hometown of Kenji Miyazawa, and eked out a life, if one could call it that, by growing our own vegetables, such as burdock, taro and sweet potatoes. It was then that Konrad and I became vegetarians. Maybe I've lived to be a hundred and two thanks to the war, who knows.

'I stayed in the cottage, looking after our three-year-old daughter, Nadezhda. She was not at all well. She didn't thrive, as we used to say. She died on the 11th of February 1942, just before her fourth birthday.

'Konrad was away a lot. I suspected that he was working for the Japanese secret police or something. He was making contact with the few foreigners who had remained in northern Japan during the war. After a while I didn't see him for more than a few days in the span of half a year, or longer. He didn't even come back when little Nadezhda died. I had to bury her myself behind our cottage.

'It may sound strange to you that I felt so close to him, so madly in love with him, even though we spent such little time together. But that's the way we were. Whenever he came back we talked and talked the whole night. Oh, there was more than talking. But women my age don't dwell on those things. I'll leave that up to your imagination, Abby.'

I picked up my mobile phone and pressed the screen to stop the recording of the interview I had done with her in Kobe. It was 10:29, and light was streaming into my bedroom through an opening in the curtains.

My back and shoulders were aching. I had not budged from the spot for over an hour. I felt pains, like needles in a sewing machine going up and down into the pit of my stomach. I would have to eat something. The coffee I had drunk seemed like acid sitting in my bowel. I went into the kitchen, opened the refrigerator and took out a large tub of plain yoghurt. I removed the lid. As I pulled the foil top off, blobs of yoghurt shot out onto my kaftan. I rubbed them off with my forefinger and sucked my fingertips. I took a soupspoon from the drawer beside the sink and ate the entire tub of yoghurt, only pausing to breathe in between rapid scoops. I put the tub and spoon in the sink, returned to my desk and resumed the recording.

'Konrad sent me letters from time to time. The envelopes were addressed in beautiful Japanese script. He said that after the war we would go to some country like Australia or New Zealand "where they know nothing about our past or anybody else's" and he would teach calligraphy to children. He was an amazing man, Abby. There's a difference between women of my generation and yours. We defined ourselves on the basis of the successes of our men. We didn't have the breathing space to consider whether this was right or wrong. It was simple reality. You are free to define yourselves on the merits of your own life. I envy you that, Abby.'

'Yeah,' I heard myself saying to her, 'you're right, Maria. We are so much freer to be ourselves than you were in your life and times.'

I knew that I had said something else to her after that but can't recall what … probably some polite cliché. I quickly turned the recording off again. It was already 11:42 and the article had to be emailed to Mr Murota by 13:00. And I hadn't written a single line!

Should I just write it up as a straight interview, with my questions in italics and her answers in between? No, I hated articles like that. I needed to understand her and the age in which she lived. Without that what would my role in this be? I would be irrelevant. Not even a medium, just air between her life and the readers'. I stared at the blank Word document. I held my open hands over the keyboard. They were waiting to strike. But no finger would descend onto a key. It was as if my hands were ceramic, a sculpture suspended in air. I reached for the mobile phone on my lap and restarted the recording, skipping over my own words to get to hers.

'Everything went along like that, you see, until Konrad was arrested in January 1945. The police left me alone. They did come to interrogate me once, but my Japanese wasn't very good then. I led them to Nadezhda's grave behind the cottage and told them, gesturing and speaking in broken Japanese, about her. They saluted me and left.

'I stayed on at that cottage for several years after the war ended. The farmers in the district were very kind to me. They brought me all the vegetables I could eat. One of them was particularly kind. His name was Hideo Negishi. He was five years younger than me. He was teaching himself Russian so that he could read Pushkin and Esenin and Tolstoy in the original. I started tutoring him once in a while. As his home was far away, sometimes he would stay over at my cottage. The trains at that time were not so reliable in that part of Japan. People called it "The Japanese Tibet".

'One evening he asked me if I ever got lonely. I told him that even though Konrad and I had been separated since the time of the war, I felt as though I carried him inside me. That's how strong my love for him was. I was devoted to him, Abby. Devoted. Do you understand that?'

'Not really,' I had said.

'Be that as it may, one night … well, Hideo was sitting next to me on the sofa. It's this sofa, the one we are sitting on now. I kept it all these years. He slowly lowered his head and rested it in my lap, and I began stroking his hair. I had Konrad in my mind, but I was feeling a deep rush of emotion for Hideo. Suddenly the time shared by me and Konrad was deleted. It was as if all of my love and passion for Konrad was being channelled towards Hideo. I even forgot about my little daughter. I could only see Hideo's beautiful face. He was looking up at me. You know, Abby, I think he was in love with me. It would be impossible for you to picture that now, but I was once rather pretty. At least people said I was.'

'No, I can see that. What happened?'

'You mean, between Hideo and me?'

'Yes.'

'You're not going to write this in your article, are you? This sort of thing is embarrassing to people of my generation.'

'No. Of course I won't include it.'

'Well, what happened, you ask. Well, Hideo and I made love. It was his very first time. And I had never known any man other than Konrad. It wasn't like women of your generation where everyone's been with everyone else. Anyway, well, what can I say? It was beautiful, Abby, beautiful for both of us. We made love right here on this sofa, Abby. Hideo was lying where you are sitting now. Hideo had a beautiful body. I would say it was the body of an Adonis, if it doesn't sound incongruous that a Japanese body could be like an ideal Greek one. Do you understand?'

'Not really. I'm not sure what an Adonis is, actually.'

'But then the disaster struck.'

'Disaster?'

'Yes.'

'What do you mean?'

'Konrad, who I had not seen for months, came home. I had assumed that they tortured and killed him.'

'You mean, he came back when you and Hideo were making love?'

'Just after. We were both naked. It was the middle of summer. We were still covered in sweat. Hideo had fallen asleep, dear boy, with his head right here in my lap. And, in an instant, Konrad was standing in the doorway.'

'Oh my God.'

'That's just what I said, except in Russian, *O, bozhe moi!*'

'What did he do?'

'Who, Konrad?'

'Yes. Yes, Konrad.'

'He just turned around and walked right back out the door without saying a word. Poor Hideo, who had woken up, didn't know whether to cover his genitals or his face with his hands. I think he put one hand over each. One trouble was that when he woke up his … his … member was … standing. I think he must have been dreaming of me. This made it hard for him to hide himself entirely with one hand. I didn't budge the whole time. I mean, I was sitting right here where I am sitting now, Abby.

'You see, for Konrad I was a possession. He could go away and come back knowing that I would still be his and his alone. Seeing me like that made him realise that I didn't belong to him. I may have been devoted to him, as I said to you, but I wasn't his to do with what he liked. I was my own woman, Abby. I always was and still am. You see, I had chosen to be devoted to him out of love. But I also loved Hideo. Can you understand that?'

'I think so. What did Hideo do after that?'

'After that? He got married to me, that's what he did. Konrad and I had never been officially married. We lived in a big house owned for generations by Hideo's family in Morioka. And we had four children, Abby. They're living all over the world. Not one is here in Japan. I have eleven grandchildren and seven great-grandchildren all together. My youngest daughter, who is now in her late fifties, married a Russian and lives in St. Petersburg. She has long wanted me to visit her there. But, you know, I never really went to Russia proper. I only knew Harbin, which is now in China, as a child. I wouldn't fit in there. I fit in here, in Japan.

'Hideo and I moved here to Kobe about forty years ago. He had never lived on the sea. You know, he became a famous translator of Russian poetry into Japanese. His Russian was far better than mine in the end. He taught Russian at Osaka University of Foreign Studies.'

'Did he … I mean, when did he …?'

'… die?'

'Yes.'

'Last year, at age ninety-six. I never thought that I would outlive him … my beautiful Japanese Adonis. As for Konrad, he disappeared completely out of my life. I have no idea what became of him. He no doubt went back to the Soviet Union. If he did, Stalin's men would have sent him to the Gulag for sure.'

That's where the recording ended. Maria had said that she was feeling tired and couldn't go on any further. I told her that I had sufficient material for the article, which was going to be about the life and times in the old days for an émigré woman in Japan.

'But all this that I told you is so personal,' she said, as I stood in the spacious entryway of her home in the well-to-do Kobe suburb of James Yama. 'Surely it won't tell anyone about what life was like for others.'

'It will,' I assured her. 'I'll try to convey something of what I've heard today so that readers can see themselves in your life.'

'Have you been able to do that, Abby?' she asked.

'Me? Not really. But maybe I can do it for others.'

I slumped forward, crossing my arms and resting my head on the keyboard. This sent a long line of random letters onto the first two lines of the document on the screen.

'That's the rub,' I said to myself aloud, looking up at the screen. 'Total gobbledygook. Not a word that will make sense to anyone coming out of you, Abby Eisenglass. Not a fucking word. Just random letters made by your head. Story of my life.'

I shut my eyes and rested my head on my arms. Beads of sweat were forming on my forehead, and a pain was gnawing the walls of my stomach, becoming more and more intense. My stomach felt like it was a pit full of foul liquid. I was sure that if I looked down at it, that's what I would see: a pit full of the foul liquid of my own making.

I stared at the computer screen through closed lids. A faint white blank light filtered through them. I was unaware of what time it was. But I was sure that if I looked at my digital clock it would be past 13:00 … past my deadline and not a recognisable word out of me. I kept pressing down hard on the keys with my forearms until an entire page was covered with letters and signs.

I knew precisely what I wanted to say, but simply did not know how to order those letters and signs into something that had meaning for me.

The Returnee

The principal rose from his folding chair on the brightly lit stage, approached the podium and bowed, first to the middle-aged woman who had been seated beside him and then to the audience that filled the auditorium.

'Can everyone hear me?' he said, leaning heavily into the microphone on the podium before moving it a few centimetres closer to his mouth and standing erect. He paused for a long moment, as if not knowing what to say. Two or three people coughed in the back section, where the relatives of the graduates had been placed. Some of the more than two hundred and fifty graduates fidgeted, as if uncomfortable with their fingers.

'I want to congratulate all of our graduates today,' said the principal. 'In a matter of weeks you will be going out into the world, most of you, I am proud to say, on to universities in this and other cities of Japan. I am proud of you all. It is thanks to you and those graduates who have preceded you that the name of Chuo High School is known throughout the country as a school that produces first-class men—and a few women, I hasten to add—who have contributed to the great economic achievements of the postwar era. Thank you, boys … and girls. Japan may soon be number one in the world, and I want you each in his own way to be number one as well. With you at the helm, the Japanese ship of state will take the lead!'

The adults, who occupied the back half of the auditorium, broke out into applause, which the principal acknowledged by bowing once again.

'Thank you very much,' he said, looking over the heads of the graduates. 'Needless to say, the economic miracle of the past decade has been no miracle, literally speaking. It has been accomplished thanks to the fathers—and, I hasten to add, mothers—of Japan who have sacrificed everything to raise the ... the, uh, gross, the gross national product of this country to such heights while managing to produce such accomplished graduates in the bargain. I am particularly moved to see so many fathers here today. Thank you, fathers, for giving up your valuable time at work to celebrate Japan's new generation of high achievers!

'We heard earlier from the valedictorian of the class, who amazingly is a female—as I have always said, girls can often approach the level of their male counterparts with the right kind of encouragement—Kataoka Emiko. Emiko, as you heard, delivered her speech in English. This is a first for Chuo High. I myself did once deliver an address in English, uh, some years ago now, for a graduation ceremony. But, as you all know, I am fluent in the language, as my many American friends have remarked to me ... or, well, rather fluent, that is, uh, somewhat fluent.

'But, putting myself aside for the time being, Emiko has been awarded a full scholarship to Keio University in Tokyo, where she will be pursuing her studies in international relations. Someday in the distant future, some of you young people may see a female being made prime minister of our country or, at the very least, the president of one of our major companies. Do not be surprised if that person turns out to be Kataoka Emiko's own daughter! Now, I would like to ask the parents of Kataoka Emiko to stand so that you may all personally acknowledge them and their achievement in producing her.'

The principal scanned the back rows, searching for Kataoka Emiko's parents. A number of graduates turned around in their chairs and raised their heads above the others. Finally a man in a dark suit and striped grey necktie reluctantly stood and immediately sat down again. A woman in her fifties rushed across the stage from the wings and whispered into the principal's ear.

'My secretary has just informed me,' he said, 'that Mrs Kataoka is indisposed. I am so sorry to hear that. She must be very proud of her daughter, nevertheless.'

The principal cleared his throat and appeared at a loss for what to say. He glanced at his secretary, who had already retreated safely to the wings. She stretched her palm out in the direction of the middle-aged woman sitting on stage.

'Oh yes, of course. Before we adjourn to the courtyard where you will be able to take photographs of your sons and daughters to mark this momentous day, Mrs Muroyama has requested to have a few words with you. Please give her your undivided attention.'

The principal took three steps backwards, gesturing for Mrs Muroyama to go to the podium. She slowly rose from her seat and stood in front of it, running her gaze over both the graduates and the relatives seated behind them.

A tall woman, she was dressed in a long black-and-white polka dot Marimekko dress. She walked to the podium and gripped its sides with both hands before half-turning to the principal and bowing. She then returned her gaze to the audience, this time moving it gradually from right to left, in order to make eye contact with as many mothers and fathers of the graduates as she could. Being taller than the principal, she loosened the handle on the microphone and raised it to the level of her lips.

'Good afternoon, mothers, fathers and relatives of the graduates … and good afternoon, graduates,' she said in a strong clear voice.

Many of the graduates and their relatives mumbled a 'good afternoon' to her in return. She paused for some fifteen or twenty seconds. She turned to the principal, who was now seated back in his chair. He thought of smiling and nodding in order to encourage her, but her long silence had made him feel strangely tense. He sat up straight in his chair and stared above the heads of the people in the audience, striking, in his own mind, a noble pose.

Mrs Muroyama cleared her throat. She produced a sheet of folded paper from the single pocket of her dress. She unfolded the sheet, looked it over once with pursed lips and put it down.

'Last night I wrote down a few words that I planned to say to you today. But suddenly I feel it inappropriate to be formal at this moment, though I know full well that these ceremonies rely on a rather strict formality to maintain their decorum. I do know some of you parents and quite a few students as well, classmates of my son Takeshi.'

She paused for a moment and glanced at the sheet of paper on the podium as if considering reading it out. There was some comfort in predetermined words. It was almost as if they comprised an official report of what had transpired, a report that would be objective, compassionless and acceptable to all.

Again there was a prolonged silence. Some people in the audience were beginning to feel visibly uncomfortable. Beads of sweat appeared on the principal's brow, though, it being March, there was still a distinct chill in the auditorium air.

'I'm so sorry,' she finally said. 'Coming here today has not been easy for me, as you can imagine. My husband is still in Seattle. His company would not allow him time off to come to his son's graduation, given the circumstances.'

The principal twisted his wrist and glanced down at his watch. It was already three minutes past two. The ceremony was scheduled to end precisely at two. The vice principal had warned him that it would not be a good idea to permit Mrs Muroyama to speak. He should have listened to him. But, due to the unusual turn of events of the past school year, he felt he had had no choice. 'It's the human thing to do,' he had told his vice principal. 'We can't exactly deny her this single opportunity to appear before us.'

Mrs Muroyama unscrewed the microphone from its handle and, holding onto it, stepped forward to the edge of the stage. The black wire, just long enough to reach the distance, cut a taut line between the microphone in her hand and the handle fixed to the podium. The principal's brow was now streaming with sweat. He removed a white handkerchief from the side pocket of his jacket and blotted his brow. Some of the graduates exchanged glances, aware that the ceremony was going minutes over time and wondering how long they would be required to remain seated.

'I apologise for taking up everyone's time,' said Mrs Muroyama, now standing with her toes over the edge of the stage. 'I won't be long. I just want you to know about your fellow graduate, Muroyama Takeshi, my … son.'

She turned to one side and took a few steps in an arc, as if the microphone's wire was the arm of a compass keeping her a set distance from the podium.

'My husband was, some eight years ago, transferred by his company to the United States. As you know, the accepted practice in Japanese companies is for the man to go abroad alone and for the wife to stay with the children or child in Japan for the sake of their education. But my husband would not have that. He insisted that our son, Takeshi, and I accompany him to Seattle. "He'll learn English like a native", my husband said, "and when we go back to Japan get a great job in one of the big trading companies". I was worried that Takeshi would lose the friends he was making in primary school, but my husband said, "He'll make new friends. Seattle has a lot of Japanese people living in it. He won't be alone. I promise". He promised our son that he would thrive in America and have a bright future in Japan.

'Well, it was true. Takeshi was amazing. After two or three months he was not only speaking English like an American but acting like one too. My husband was a bit worried because Takeshi seemed to rebel against anything he said. But, after all, his American friends were saying awful things about their parents. Takeshi just wanted to fit in, I told my husband. He'll go back to being a regular Japanese teenager when we get back home. Takeshi's the quiet type, self-effacing. He'll fit right in in Japan, too. After all, it's his home, isn't it? That's what I thought at the time, even if I didn't put it into so many words.'

She turned her back on the audience and, for a few seconds, stared at the principal. His brow was now glistening in sweat. He held his handkerchief against it and grinned at her, lowering his eyes and subtly pointing to his watch with his forefinger.

'I see that the principal is giving me a sign,' said Mrs Muroyama, making an about-face at the edge of the stage and inadvertently pulling on the wire, which nearly dislodged from the podium, rendering the microphone useless. A young female technician immediately dashed out of the wings, handed her a handheld microphone and, bowing as she ran, disappeared back where she came from.

'Thank you. I won't be long, ladies and gentlemen … and dear graduates. Perhaps I do not need to tell many of you what happened when we returned to Kyoto about a year ago. I think you already know. My husband and I wanted Takeshi to graduate a distinguished high school such as this one so that he could bring himself up to the level of all of you and pass the entrance exam of a first-class Japanese university. My husband could not leave his job in Seattle. Takeshi returned home with me. He returned … home.'

She paused for a moment, unsure how to proceed from there. Then she slowly brought the microphone down to her side and, gripping its handle tightly, continued to speak to the graduates and their relatives in a loud and firm voice.

'But, as some of you are all too well aware, from his very first days here at Chuo High School, Takeshi was deliberately isolated by his classmates. Though they themselves were struggling to say simple everyday phrases in English, they—no, you—teased him mercilessly for every little mistake he made in Japanese. He tried to cover it up with humour—what he himself called "goofing around"—but that only increased the hostility you dealt out to him. I phoned my husband and told him what was happening, but he said, "Look, it's what happens in all schools. It will build his character. Let him deal with it by himself. For God's sake, don't complain to the school. It will only make things worse". By things he meant the bullying.

'Well, dear graduates and parents, I did complain to the school, especially when they asked me why Takeshi was not showing up in class some days and when … when … he began harming himself by putting sharp pencils in his ears until his eardrums bled.'

The graduates and their relatives sat perfectly still. The principal rose to his feet and took a step forward; but Mrs Muroyama, sensing his approach from behind, put the microphone back to her lips and said, 'Just a minute or two more, please.' The principal stopped, turned around and returned to his seat, dabbing his forehead with the handkerchief. He started to put the wet handkerchief back in his side pocket, but clutched it between his knees instead.

'I begged Takeshi to stick it out until graduation. I told him that he could go to university in California or anywhere in the States that he wished. But he said, "Mom, I'm a Japanese, so I've got to be successful here in Japan". He believed what his father had said to him.

'He wanted to be successful. He did try. He joined a club. He refused to speak English, even in English class. For one thing, I think he didn't want to embarrass the teacher. He was a considerate boy, my son. He always thought of others before himself. Over the closing months of last year he withdrew into himself more and more. But he still managed to leave home on most days and get to school. He finished the course and was looking forward to this graduation very much. He wanted to be one of you. That's all he wanted … to be one of all of you.'

Once again she held the microphone to her side. For some reason, she bent down, picked up the wire attached to the other microphone and pulled it until it stretched on an angle across the top of her dress.

'Some of the boys who are sitting right here in this auditorium,' she continued, 'who are listening to these very words and who are graduating today, found out that Takeshi was harming himself with a pencil. So they took him to the edge of the playground one day when he had stayed late at school for club activity, threw him down on the gravel and said, "Show us what you do with a pencil! Is it a hard pencil? Is it as hard as ....?" I ... I ... I'm sorry.'

The principal once again rose and approached her from the back. He was about to reach out to her, to take the microphone from her side, but she snapped her head sharply in his direction. Twisting the black wire around her wrist, she gradually lifted the hand microphone to her lips and said in a whisper, 'As you all know, all you graduates and you parents and other relatives, ten days ago my son Takeshi took his own life. He hanged himself in his bedroom. There is nothing else I want to say today. Congratulations to you all. May your dreams come true. May Japan continue to prosper because of you. May you all have successful lives ... a successful ... life.'

She unravelled the wire and dropped it, with the hand microphone, onto the floor. The thud echoed through the loudspeakers on either side of the stage. She stepped down the stairs at the front of the stage and walked up the aisle. Not a single graduate or relative looked at her as she made her way to the back of the auditorium. They all sat in silence with heads bowed until she was no longer among them.

The principal picked up the microphone and rapped its head with the knuckle of his middle finger. Several loud taps were heard coming from the speakers.

'Uh ... I, uh ... I apologise, I mean, for going over our time limit, and ... well, please stand and make your way into the courtyard for commemorative photographs to mark this wonderful day for the graduates of Chuo High School, class of 1967. Producing young high achievers as you are, I feel as though the future of our country will be bright. Remember, be number one. Remember, in whatever you do, do your utmost! That is the thought I want you to take home with you today.

'Many years from now, when you look back on this day, I hope you will return in your thoughts to the school that gave you your chance ... gave you your future life.'

The principal dropped the microphone to his side and stood perfectly still. His forehead was now dry and he was shivering from the cold.

He stared blankly over the heads of the graduates. As for the graduates and their relatives, they simply marched in two very straight lines into the sun.

The Return of Lafcadio Hearn

I PASSED AWAY IN TOKYO IN THE YEAR 1904 AND HERE I AM BACK again in the good old town well over a century later.

Now, as one grows older—and I am now pushing one hundred and seventy—one acquires a perspective on things. You might argue that one hundred and seventy is too old to judge the world. But I'm sure you'll agree that art is in perspective, not statistics. And I can see all the way to and beyond the horizon. It may be the horizon that's behind us all now, but it is a horizon nonetheless. Why do people always think of the horizon as a thing in front of them? The one behind us, I would argue, is just as important, if not more so.

I was born in 1850 on a Greek island. Some of my biographers have referred to it as a 'small' Greek island. Well, I defy them to find one that isn't. Throughout my life I was more intimately bound to my ruffian imagination than to the rules of my century's decorum, more titillated and intrigued by ghosts than by so-called real people.

So you see, it is perfectly natural that I should be coming back like this 'from over the horizon' after the passing of many generations.

When it came to the nonliving I was always at home. I was smack into my element. But I wouldn't ever call myself 'morbid'. Edgar Allan Poe, now he was morbid! I wasn't at all like Poe, though I did once name one of my cats after him.

I spent a total of fourteen years in Japan. These, in fact, corresponded to the final fourteen years of my life. And while I did witness the Sino-Japanese War of 1894-95 and the beginning of the Russo-Japanese War in 1904, I missed out on the Great Kanto Earthquake of 1923 and World War II, not to mention World War One and conveyor belt sushi.

Naturally I know that the first thing you are dying to ask me is, 'Has Japan changed a lot since the time you were last here?'

Well, to tell you the truth, the answer is 'no', although some places like train stations are a bit more crowded than they used to be, and there were no airports, especially when you take into account the fact that the first flying machine didn't even get off the ground until the year before I died. And we didn't have fax machines in our houses then, though, to be fair, neither do you now; and we knew nothing of what is enigmatically called 'reality television'. Okay, we may not have had television at all, but let me tell you we knew reality when we saw it, which is a lot more than I can say for some of these people I've seen here since I got back. As for fake news, in my day most news was fake, so don't go thinking that everything is invented in the future.

Yet some things, I must admit, really have changed. I used to be able to get from my home in Tokyo to the university where I taught in under an hour, thanks to the speed and strength of the rickshaw runners who propelled me. Yesterday I took the very same route so that I could report to you on the difference; and it took me longer to cover the distance, despite the fact that the vehicle transporting me came courtesy of a conveyancer called 'Uber'. So much for improvements in people's command of the German language!

I lived for some months, way back in 1890, in the lovely Japan Sea coastal town of Matsue, subsequently moving to the old castle town of Kumamoto in Kyushu. In both places I taught English to youngsters. The mid years of the last decade of the nineteenth century found me in the international port city of Kobe, where I worked as a newspaper man until transferring to Tokyo to take up a position as instructor, once again in the English language, at Tokyo Imperial University, which is now, for some reason that I, as well as certain politicians, cannot fathom, referred to without mentioning the capitalised adjective in the middle. Much to my surprise, I learned that the country known as 'The United Kingdom' still boasts an Imperial College and an Imperial War Museum in its capital, so what's the big deal? It just goes to show that some countries can lose their empire and entertain the luxury of pretending that they haven't.

Not long after my return I travelled back to Matsue and Kumamoto, curious to see if my teaching of English had had any effect on the young people who study the language there.

I tell you, it gives me no joy to divulge here that their grasp of the language was no firmer than that of my own pupils some one hundred and twenty-odd years ago. Furthermore, the English words printed on their 'T' shirts and 'sweat' shirts were barely comprehensible. I am the first to admit that being away for over a century certainly does date a man's vocabulary. But what, I ask you, does 'Trump's Tweets Uploaded to the iCloud' mean? Can this be English?

Oh, I can hear you saying, 'He's just an old fuddy-duddy Greek-Irish ghost story writer who's kvetching about everything new.' I don't mind. Wait till you get to be a hundred and seventy and see what people say about you! I actually pride myself on keeping abreast of things Japanese, though these past weeks have presented me with a most precipitous learning curve.

I soon realised that the best way to get to the bottom on the other side of that steep arc of knowledge and catch up with people in Japan was to go straight to the nation's capital, Tokyo, and live life for myself. Thanks to my books having become known here and my being a foreigner, I was immediately able to land a job teaching English at a wonderful privately-owned educational institution, The Shinjuku Center for English Study and Placement of Sons and Daughters Who Cannot Get into a Good Japanese University in American Junior Colleges Homestay Institute, or TSCESPSDWCGGJUAJCHI for short.

I started by requiring my students to buy my own books as texts for my classes, which is apparently standard practice employed by professors at Japanese universities to stop their books from going out of print. This afforded me a modest but steady income and allowed me to set myself up in a tiny flat which people incongruously referred to as a 'mansion'.

My students were, without exception, as diligent and capable as the ones I taught back in the late nineteenth and early twentieth centuries. They all used 'mobile' devices late into the night and sent me their essays 'by finger' ... or, as they said, in admirable usage of the Latin-derived word, 'digitally'. My best student, a young woman named Mimi Hoichi, quickly mastered spoken English under my tutelage, primarily by ear.

'The gleanings which I have heretofore possessed,' she told me, 'thanks to you, Dear Professor, shall, I daresay, remain with me for all my born days. Oh they are no mere apparitions, I can vouchsafe you that.'

Now honestly, have you ever heard such flowing English spoken by a Japanese as that? Even your so-called native speakers of the language are incapable of exercising vocabularic (oh yes, it's a word, despite the fact that 'spellcheck' refuses to recognise it) feats with such exalting proficiency. *Res ipsa loquitur.* And if you don't know what that means, you're more of a schnook than I thought you were.

I encountered a young Englishman working in a stock and bond company in Tokyo. I was pleased to see the ample whiskers covering cheek and chin, and the thick braces holding up his trousers. I conveyed to him what Mimi Hoichi had told me.

'Yeah, I get where she's coming from,' he said, 'but it's a creepy way to put it.'

Being an old horror story aficionado, I was tickled by his usage of the word 'creepy', but nonplussed by the rest of it.

'So how would you *put* it?' I asked him.

'I'd say, "Thanks prof, learned heaps, awesome".'

'Awesome?'

'Yeah. Awesome.'

I was happy to see that at least something was inspiring awe in young people. He waved goodbye and hopped onto a moving staircase, disappearing on the floor above.

This contraption intrigued me, so I hopped onto one of its corrugated stairs myself. When I reached the landing atop this stair-continuum I saw something that radically altered my opinion of this new Japan.

I stood before a door made of glass. On this door were words in Latin and English: VIDEO AND DVD RENTAL.

I deciphered this title immediately, though it be a curious combination of the two languages. I am sure that I do not need to tell you that, translated, this means 'I SEE AND 500-5-500 RENTAL'.

I wondered, in all innocence, what I would see on the other side of this mysterious glass door that opened of its own accord as I approached it. Here I had written such bizarre and eerie tales as 'Snow Woman' and 'Story of a Fly', yet who was this person, I asked myself, with the imagination to come up with a room where so many visions could be rented?

Once inside, I was drawn, as if by some magnetic force, to the section of 500-5-500s marked under the heading 'Classics', overjoyed to see the works of some of my most esteemed Victorian contemporaries such as Victor Hugo and Herman Melville represented there, not to mention those by Émile Zola, Sir Walter Scott and a few dubious Roman epics such as 'Spartacus' and 'Roman Holiday' of which I had never heard. What puzzled me, however, was that all of these works appeared to be of the exact same length. Adjacent shelves carried even smaller 'discs' in little translucent boxes that were called '400s'.

Next door to this highly educational I See and 500-5-500 Rental establishment was an enterprise with an even more esoteric and respectable name: Discotheque. Though my Greek was a tad rusty due to the fact that I was only two years old when I left the country, and that being more than a hundred and sixty years ago, I immediately recognised this reference to 'a place where platters are stored'. I had always been inordinately fond of Japanese ceramics and was eager to enter this discotheque and see if I could pick up a bargain.

What I learned, however, had little to do with quaint mud kilns or colourful dripping glazes. This strangely misnamed 'discotheque' was crowded with young people who were wriggling and gyrating to a raucous blast of noise coming seemingly out of nowhere. One of the wriggling and gyrating youths was a Japanese; and it wasn't long before I found myself wriggling and gyrating about in a similar fashion and having a most stimulating tete-a-tete, in fits and shouts, with him. He turned out to be a student at Waseda University, where I myself had occupied a teaching position, my last, way back on that other side of the old horizon.

'Lafcadio Hearn, eh?' said the Japanese youth in English. 'Funny, the name rings a bell. Hey, I remember. You're the dude who wrote all about the old Japan and how much you hated everything becoming so modern and Western, right? I thought you were a goner, Laf-baby. I mean, didn't you bite the dust, like, ages ago? Kick the bucket like the dinosaurs?'

There was much to warm the cockles of an old living fossil's heart in what he said, particularly in his calling me a 'dude' and in his use of the phrase 'ages ago'. I like things that happened ages ago. I mean, what is the present if not a moment ensuring that the past does the right thing by time?

But why did he call me 'Laf-baby'? Could he be thinking that I have come back to Earth as someone born again? Am I in reality a kind of newborn?

I could not hear this young man well over the din that I now realised was emanating from little black boxes hanging from the ceiling.

'You seem to speak English very proficiently,' I hollered at him.

'Thanks, man,' he hollered back. 'I went to Truman High in Silicon Valley. I'll message you on Facebook. Well, be seein' you, man. Ciao.'

And with that the young man writhed away from me with an expression of excruciating pain on his face. In fact, everyone there seemed to display this expression on his face; yet all and sundry also seemed to be enjoying themselves at the same time. Could it be that the works of my esteemed French predecessor, the Marquis de Sade, had experienced a revival in Japan?

Well, all that happened some time ago now.

At first I couldn't figure out for the life of me what 'True Man High in Silicon Valley' meant. It made no more sense than 'Trump's Tweets Uploaded to the iCloud'. And I knew what a hand book was, but what is a face book? But since then, fanatic grubber that I am—or was—I have gone to the local bibliotheque and perused an encyclopaedia that was miraculously squeezed into a single 400. I think if you met me today you would find that I am a real hepcat, a neat groovy swinger when it comes to all things that we, as humans, dig. You see, I am determined never again to be out of date, not now and certainly not in the foreseeable future either. (I hate that term, 'foreseeable future', as if such a thing ever existed.)

As a result of my return to Japan in the twenty-first century I have attained a kind of present-day Enlightenment; and, in the process, I have become all too aware that I am no longer in a position to write about this country. Japan may not have changed all that much since I was last here, but I most definitely have.

As such, this is, I am afraid, the last thing that I shall write about Japan or about anywhere, for that matter, for a long time … who knows, perhaps even for another century or two.

But rest assured, if not in peace, yourself. You have not seen the last of me or my ilk.

I leave you with this, my last and most original *bon mot*: 'I shall return' … in one form or another.

Don't do anything I can't do … Man.

A Certain Utopia

THE MOST BIZARRE THING HAPPENED. I DISCOVERED A DOCUMENT in the form of diary entries written in the early Meiji era by my great-great-great-grandmother.

It is fortunate that I have such an unusual surname. If I were a Suzuki or a Sato or a Yamaguchi, tracing an ancestor would be an impossible task. But I was able to find a reference to the diary on the internet thanks to its appearance under my unique surname. The diary has been kept in a small wooden box in the National Diet Library in Tokyo.

There are almost no people in Japan with the surname of Tsuiri. Tsuiri is written with three characters: 'chestnut', 'flower' and 'fall'. The name's pronunciation is an abbreviation of 'tsuyu-iri', or 'the start of the rainy season', or when the chestnut flowers fall.

The fact that the name originates in Hyogo prefecture is a link to the place where my great-great-great-grandmother wrote her diary, the village of Tachikui, in the middle of that prefecture. It seems that she lived for a short time in a Utopian community in that village. But I am getting ahead of myself....

When the feudal period ended in 1868 and the modern era of Meiji began, most Japanese people didn't have surnames. Being primarily farmers, they naturally took on names borrowed from the seasons or the land around them, or both: Akiyama (autumn mountain), Haruno (spring field), Tani (valley), Yamamoto (the foot of the mountain), Nishikawa (river to the west), Tanaka (in the paddies), and so on.

My ancestors devised their surname from a season in an ingenious way. The people of Hyogo prefecture, where Kobe was and still is the main port, celebrated the falling of the chestnut flowers from their trees with a festival. This festival was held as a communal prayer for the rains to come and make the rice crop bountiful. My ancestor Tsuiri Su-e, however, rejected this indigenous tradition and escaped into a world totally unlike that known to and practised by her people up to then.

But before I go into the details of her life as a young woman, as set out in her remarkable diary, I must tell you how I came to search for it in the first place.

My father knew nothing at all of my family's distant past and frankly was not in the least interested in hearing about it after I had uncovered the diary. Neither was his mother, my grandmother.

'I have no idea how your grandfather or his descendants got his unusual surname,' she wrote me in an email when I offered to scan the diary and send it to her. 'You should be concentrating on computer studies or economics or something useful like that, not some old thing written a hundred and fifty years ago. Scan me your grades from your university courses, that's what grandma wants to see!'

As for me, I too had no interest whatsoever in my family's past until I went to Australia for a homestay in the summer of my second year at university. The family I stayed with were Polish, or actually of Polish descent. No one in the family spoke Polish or had ever been to Poland. But the Krzyzewskis—I can spell it but I'll never be able to pronounce it!—had done a search on a website dedicated to finding out about family history. At the dinner table they were often talking about their 'roots'.

I didn't know what they meant by 'roots'; and when they asked me about mine, I just said, 'I'm Japanese.'

'We know that, Eiko,' said Mr Krzyzewski, 'but where do your people come from?'

'Japan.'

'We know that! But where in Japan?' he said, putting down his cloth napkin, folding it on the table and ironing it with his palm. 'Who were they? What did they do?'

I hadn't a clue about those things. All I knew was that I was a Japanese with an unusual name. I didn't think we Japanese had roots. Well, I knew we had ancestors and all that, but I didn't think they had anything to do with me and Japan in the year 2020.

So when I returned to Tokyo from Melbourne at the end of August I decided to do some research into my roots. The internet led me to the National Diet Library at Nagatacho in downtown Tokyo.

The morning of the very first day I spent at the library, the computerised files showed up a document under my name, Tsuiri, located in the archive stacks in a numbered crate of materials related to the history of Hyogo prefecture between 1868 and 1875. I requested the document, and in less than thirty minutes, had it in my hand.

But the problem was, I couldn't read it. It was written by brush and India ink in a cursive script that I could not decipher. I wonder if in a hundred and fifty years from now people won't be able to access our computer files and not comprehend what we are writing now.

I asked the librarian if there was anyone who could help me read the diary. Luckily, one of the casual staff, a student of Japanese history at Gakushuin University, happened to be there that morning. He offered to help me read the diary. It was a doubly fortunate encounter for me, because the student, Kobayashi Jun, is just the most cool and awesome guy I've ever met and we are now seeing each other at least two nights a week. Thank you great-great-great-grandma!!!!

'Your ancestor's awesome,' said Jun that first morning, running his eyes up and down the lines as he excitedly unravelled the thin rice paper scroll of the diary. 'This is an amazing historical document that should be looked into and published. Can I copy this ... uh, what was your name? Can I ask that?'

'Tsuiri.'

'Pardon?'

'Tsuiri. Tsuiri Eiko.'

'Can I call you Eiko?'

'Sure, it's okay.'

'I'm Jun. Oh, you can see my surname on the badge. But call me Jun.'

'Okay.'

He read the entire diary while I sat beside him in the spacious reading room of the library. When he came to the end of the scroll, he just shook his head, saying, 'Awesome, awesome' over and over again.

'Is it a diary?' I asked. 'I can tell that it has entries that are dated. Oh, hang on, I just got an SMS.'

I took my mobile phone from my handbag and flipped the cover open.

'It's okay, it's nothing, just from my mother,' I said, replacing the phone in my handbag. 'So, who is it by? I mean, who wrote it?'

'It's just signed 'Su-e' at the end. But someone who put it in this wooden box, let's see, in the year Taisho 2, that would be, let's see, 1913, seemed to know the person or at least be familiar with the diary, because here, clearly written on this box, is the words "This is the diary of Tsuiri Su-e, born in the year 1853 in Kobe, having lived in Tachikui Village in the district of Tamba". It seems that your ancestor lived in some kind of Utopian community and …'

'Some kind of what?'

'A Utopian community, you know.'

'No, what's that?'

'Oh, it's when a group of people get together and go live somewhere all together and make rules about how they should ideally live. The word comes from a novel by the English writer Thomas More. They were idealists, kind of dreamers, who believed you could change human nature and that people in the future could all live in harmony with each other if they only, well, suppressed their egoism. But I think your ancestor had an ironical sense of humour because she signs the diary here at the very end with just the one character for Su-e, which is not only her name, but can also mean "the end". The end of what, I would have loved to ask her.'

Jun offered to transcribe the diary and translate it into modern Japanese for me. We exchanged emails every day after that until we met again at the library a week later. By then he had finished transcribing the diary. Both it and the transcribed printout were sitting on the table between us. He handed me the printout and thanked me.

'Why? I'm the one who should thank you,' I said.

'No. Look, Eiko, this diary has made me change the topic of my graduation thesis that I was just about to start on. I spoke with my professor and he's given permission. I'm now going to use this as a guide to how some people felt and lived in early Meiji. I can't believe it. This is so original. I'm so glad I met you, Eiko.'

'Me too.'

Perhaps he could tell by the look in my eyes that I wasn't talking solely about the diary either.

So, I record here, word for word, the diary of my great-great-great-grandmother, Tsuiri Su-e, written by her in Tachikui Village, Hyogo prefecture during the summer months of the year 1870....

THE THIRTIETH OF JUNE, THE THIRD YEAR OF MEIJI

I lay in the bed, made of pine planks with a rectangular wooden pillow, and stared at the rough ceiling for about an hour. The predawn dark gradually gave way to a greyness until there was a faint mist of light filling the room. When I began to see patterns in the swirling lines of the grain I knew I had to get up.

I am surrounded here by twenty bunks, perfectly arranged and aligned in five rows, strong and solid. There are no covers over the two windows, whose glass has ripples in it, like waves on a pond.

My only thought is, it should be time for morning chores soon. Where's that trump, that blast of sound from the horn that tells us we must get out of bed. Twenty women in one room. There's the first trump. That's the signal that the men must arise.

Now, Su-e, rise from your bunk, I tell myself. The second trump has already sounded. Get out of your bunk, throw the *haori* coat over your nightdress, over your shoulders and chest, and get yourself to the men's quarters to clean and tidy them. Sweep between the bunks with your hemp palm broom and tidy your Brothers' beds. Then go outside to the cowshed and do some milking for the breakfast. (I first tasted this thing called 'cow's milk' when I arrived here in the beginning of the month and I still find myself unable to swallow it.) It apparently will make the Brothers sturdy and strong, and what we do here we do for the Brothers, not for ourselves.

I walked slowly to the cowshed. A light rain was falling, but the rainy season, which should be upon us, had not yet begun. The meetinghouse, which was inside a dilapidated disused shrine amidst the cryptomeria trees on a raised copse, was dark inside. I bumped into a Sister.

'Excuse me,' I said.

She held her finger up to her lips and shook her head. I am still unused to not being able to speak without permission from a Brother.

Brother Jacob passed by me. The Brothers and Sisters have all taken on Christian names. Mine is Miriam, but I have trouble pronouncing it. In fact, I have trouble pronouncing all of the names used here. I turned around. Brother Jacob, bowlegged and tall for a Japanese, was staring at me as I walked to the cowshed.

As I came back from the cowshed on my way to the house with the communal dining hall in it, I passed the farmhouse where the kitchen was. Smoke was rising from in between the miscanthus reeds of the roof. The roof is in terrible disrepair. It seems that Brother Abraham, whose name was Taizo before he came here, is a reed roofer, and soon he is about to repair that roof. Brother Jacob emerged from the outhouse next to the stream and, pulling up his trousers, scowled at me, flailing his arm to get me to hurry along with my wooden bucket of cow's milk.

The Brothers were already seated in two rows at a long pine table.

The Sisters were serving them bread and grilled 'peony' meat. I had never heard of peony meat. In fact, I had never eaten any kind of animal flesh in my life before this month. Peony meat is the flesh of the wild boar. They call it by a pretty name to make it seem more palatable, that's what I think. I have to eat it, otherwise I would starve here. But every time I see a wild boar roaming around the outskirts of the village I feel sorry for it. Am I eating its soul along with its flesh? That's what I thought. But Brother Adam, who is our priest, warned that such thoughts were sinful. 'Animals don't have souls,' he said. 'Only we humans have souls.' It's different from what I was taught by my parents and grandparents, but then everything here is different.

'Japan is a new country,' said Brother Adam. 'It's like a toddler who is only three years old. The toddler has no memory of what life was like before he was born, and there is no reason why he should have. The future is entirely in his hands. Nothing that happened before now can control the motion of those hands. We must civilise the Japanese!'

He was speaking Japanese to me and he was a Japanese himself, but he said things that seemed to be coming from some foreign and unknown place outside Japan.

The dining room also serves as a schoolroom where Brother Johannes, who is our teacher, writes words from the Bible on a big board made of pine planks. We Brothers and Sisters sit on opposite sides of the room on hard chairs and repeat the words written on the planks. There are no children living here. But perhaps some will be born next year.

Tonight I sat outside and looked up at the stars. I could see the Twin Stars. I call them the Twin Sisters. I am one of those stars. I know that I have a twin somewhere, perhaps not even living now, perhaps coming into this world a long long time from now. Whoever she turns out to be, she will forever be near me, sailing across the black sky together with me, as if we were linked by some wonderful force that binds together the time between us.

The third of July, a Sunday

It was sunny and hot today. There has been no rain for three days. Sister Rachel was found praying for rain in front of the communal building because it was once a shrine and that's where she prayed as a child, in front of shrines. But Brother Adam saw her, ran up to her, lifted her up by the scruff of her neck and, pulling her head up by her long hair, slapped her hard across both cheeks. He didn't say anything, but she knew what she had done was sinful. We are allowed to pray to only one God here, the God that Brother Adam calls 'the new God of Japan'.

The largest farmhouse in the village acts as our church. The Brothers have built an altar inside it. Behind the altar there's a large cross made out of sakaki wood. This is the wood of trees that are sacred in the precincts of shrines, so I suppose the Brothers were transferring some of the holiness from what they saw as the old dead Japan to the new living one. Attached to the cross is the figure of Our Saviour Jesus Christ carved out of paulownia wood, which is strong against insects except for the longhorn beetle, so the figure of Our Saviour Jesus Christ should hopefully last a long time without being eaten, so long as the longhorn beetle doesn't get inside Him.

We all sat in the farmhouse church and sang together …

Rise oh people of Nippon
Join hands and stand together
Sing this song at the top of your voices
To your new-found land.

Praise oh praise Our Lord
Bless this land of ours
Praise oh praise Our Lord
So that the Nipponese sun will shine forever.

We said 'Amen' in unison. Then Brother Adam gave us a sermon about our sins and our salvation. He said that Japan had been a sinful land, where men and women had lived for centuries without true morality. He said that the only genuine love was the love for God Almighty, and that the love of a man for a woman or a woman for a man was evil because it diminished love for God. Jesus was celibate and so must we be. Holiness … holiness of heart, that's what matters.

I hadn't slept well the night before and fell into a light slumber during the sermon. But I have been very skilled since childhood at holding up my head whilst asleep, so, thank God, no one noticed. After the sermon we filed out of the farmhouse.

In the afternoons we have 'chatting time', during which we are allowed to talk with each other. Then we must work preparing food and making cloth, but this being a Sunday we were certainly not permitted to work. Before supper there is an hour of prayer, which we must do softly and alone beside our bunk.

After retiring for the night I couldn't get to sleep. I have been feeling very restless these past few days and don't know why.

I went outside for a walk and saw something very scandalous. Sister Ruth, whose real name was Ichiyo, was standing behind the farmhouse church, and beside her was Brother Jedidiah, whose name before he arrived here a week ago was Gozaemon. It was very dark and I was the only other person outside. He was talking to her, which he was not allowed to do after dark. Then he stood behind her. She lifted up the back of her nightdress. I could see by the light of the Milky Way, or so it seemed to me, the glowing white flesh of her thighs and buttocks. He dropped his trousers to his knees and clamped his body against hers from the back. She had her arms raised with her palms flat against the rough mud wall of the farmhouse. They didn't see me, so I quickly turned away and went inside, rushed to my bed and covered my head with my hemp blanket. But I had to uncover it because I was breathing too hard. It took me a minute before I caught my breath and could look around the room at the sleeping Sisters.

THE SEVENTH OF JULY

Brother Jedidiah and Sister Ruth have left. No one knows why (except me). This morning they were not in their bunks. They left no note to say why they left or where they went. Brother Adam was furious. 'I knew they were sinning when I saw them talking to each other, walking side by side. I should have separated and punished them both then and there.'

Brother Daniel approached me during 'chatting time' and asked if he could speak to me. I said yes.

'Why did you come here, Sister Miriam?' he asked across the table in a soft voice.

'Why?'

'Yes.'

'I am an orphan. I never found out who my parents were, whether they are alive or dead today. I was brought up by an auntie who married a man, a terrible man. He beat her every day. He was also cruel to me. But one day, in May this year, my auntie was out of the house. He came to me. I was bending down, washing bowls and chopsticks in the stream that ran behind the house. He kneeled down beside me and put his hand into the slit below the top of the sleeve of my cotton coat. Soft breast, he said, soft little nipple.'

I surprised myself that I was able to relate this to anybody, let alone a man. But my innocence does not allow me to lie. He had asked me the real reason for my coming here and I had told him. His cheek turned pale pink, like the petal of a peach blossom.

'Did I say something sinful?' I asked.

'Not to me.'

That night I went outside again, this time with Sister Mary, who, like me, was sixteen years old and also from Kobe. We knew each other from before and had played together.

'Tonight is the Tanabata Festival,' she said. 'Orihime and Hikoboshi are coming together tonight to celebrate their love.'

'It's not tonight,' I said. 'It's not for another month.'

'Oh, Su-e … no, I mean, Sister Miriam, it's now celebrated on the seventh of July, didn't you know? Tonight is the night. Oh, I wish I could be one of those stars!'

We held hands, though it was not allowed, and walked across the field under the open night sky.

But just then, without us seeing him, Brother Adam had run up to us from behind and ordered us to turn around.

'What do you think you are doing?' he demanded.

We were both so terrified that all we could do was cower before him.

'Do you realise how disgusting your behaviour is? Do you realise how uncivilised this is? Do you know anything at all? The people of Japan are barbaric children who have been running wild killing each other for centuries out of avarice and lust. Are you to be like them when you become adults? Do you two really want to be like *them*? We are doing something here that will lift our country out of the bog of deep mud that it has been in. We must change our ways if we are to live in the world as moral beings, like people in Western countries.'

The way he had called Japanese people *them* seemed so strange to me. What he was telling us was not much different from the things he said in church on Sundays. But now it was being said personally to us two, as if we were barbaric and avaricious and lustful just because we were talking and holding hands and feeling joy under an open sky, as if all the sin of Japan was residing in our two little hearts. Can that be?

THE SEVENTH OF AUGUST

I have not written in this diary for a whole month now. Before, writing things down made me feel free inside. I wanted to express something kept inside me, to record my innermost feelings, something not allowed in the 'new' Japan of this Utopia. I was longing for my invisible twin and felt I was writing everything for her.

But the daily routine of silence and obedience has begun to wear me down. I don't even have the inner strength to lift up my brush. I have felt, for a month, dead to the world.

Three more Brothers and five Sisters have left, and no new people have joined. My friend from childhood, Sister Mary, whose real name is Harue, is one of them.

'I hear that some people, even a few girls, are now leaving Japan from Kobe Port and going to Europe or America,' she said the night before she left. 'I want to escape, Su-e. I don't want to live in either the old Japan or the new one. I have a book. It's a dictionary with Japanese and English words in it. I've hid it all the time I've been here. If you want it I'll give it to you.'

'No,' I said. 'You'll need it.'

'I can get another one. My uncle who lives in Sakai has lots of books, some of them in foreign languages. I'm going to live in Sakai with him. I've written his name down here for you. Come. I'm sure he would welcome you. Sakai is a very prosperous town now. You will find work for yourself, I know.'

Brother Daniel and I have been meeting every night now behind the farmhouse. But he doesn't stand behind me and push himself against me. He is very shy and polite.

Tonight he confessed to me.

'Su-e, I am leaving tomorrow. Do you mind me calling you by your real name?'

'No.'

'I want you to come with me. My name is Michinaga. I have a surname too. It's Tsuiri.'

'What?'

'Tsuiri. It's written with the three characters for chestnut, flower and fall.'

'That's a beautiful name,' I said, walking along the wall of the farmhouse. Then I darted out into the middle of the field. The Milky Way was like a length of cotton gauze stretching from one horizon to the other. Suddenly a bright star shot across it, for an instant cutting it in half.

'Look, Su-e. A star has just crossed through the Milky Way,' said Michinaga, standing beside me.

We raised our eyes up to the sky and stood there for minutes without saying a word. This time we weren't ordered to be silent. We just felt it natural to be so.

THAT'S ALL THERE WAS OF THE DIARY. IT WAS A DIARY OF JUST FOUR entries. As Jun had said, it was signed at the end with the single character, 'Su-e'.

'That's all so sad,' I said.

'It's only fragmentary, but it gives such a vivid portrait of life in a remote village at the beginning of Meiji. We never knew of the existence of the community. After World War II many religious groups formed in Japan because of the void left in the country. People must have felt the same after the Meiji Restoration, with mixed feelings of a dread of freedom and the hope that Japanese people would reform themselves by abandoning the past and adopting a foreign morality.'

I picked up the scroll that was between us on the reading room table and unravelled it to the end.

'What's on this last page?' I asked.

'Which page?'

'Here. There's a page folded around the scroll handle. It's a normal sheet of paper, I mean, modern paper, not rice paper.'

'Oh, I didn't see that.'

'Would you read it to me?'

'Let's see. It's written in a much more legible modern script. This is ink from a fountain pen. Maybe this last page was written then and put into this very box by your great-great-great-grandmother herself. You read it, Eiko. Let's read it together.'

I pulled out the single sheet of paper wedged between the handle and the rice paper diary. This is what was written there in a script that I could easily read....

IT IS NOW OVER A YEAR SINCE EMPEROR MEIJI PASSED AWAY. Japanese people are travelling all over the world. Our industries and our armies are strong. Many Japanese people feel proud of their country. My dear friend from Tachikui Village, Harue, who died earlier this year in the city of Seattle in the state of Washington in the United States, had written me that American people love and respect us Japanese. She had married an American man and become a Christian like him. Her letter was the first one I ever saw written on a machine called a 'typewriter'. At the bottom she typed her name, Mrs Robert Everson, but above it she wrote her old name in Roman letters, Harue. She was my only childhood friend.

As for me, well, I never found God, not decades ago in Tachikui Village and not in the new Japan. But I did find love. Michinaga-san and I have been married for over forty years. I gave him twelve children, nine boys and three girls. They all survived childhood and grew up to be robust and healthy adults. I already have six grandchildren, and in the future who knows how many more children will be born and someday give birth themselves. That thought alone is all the Utopia I will ever need.

The one thing I did learn from my short stay in that village is to always ask myself what it means to be free. Is it freedom to be alone? Freedom to pray to one god or another? Freedom to disobey or defy? Or freedom to go somewhere and then leave again in search of a different kind of freedom, whatever that may mean to you.

My happiest memory from my time in Utopia came when I took myself across an open field under a sky full of the brightest stars. In the distance I heard the nighttime trump sound, calling the Japanese

Brothers and Sisters, all of whom had accepted names from the Holy Bible, to bed. I started to run as fast as I could with my eyes not on those stars but on the man waiting for me at the far end of the field....

THE LAST PAGE ENDED THERE. I PUT THE SCROLL ON THE TABLE. JUN, who had been beside me a moment ago, wasn't sitting next to me. I looked around the room for him and couldn't see him anywhere. Then I caught sight of him standing in the doorway to the National Diet Library.

The late afternoon summer light was shining behind him. All I could make out was his outline.

I carefully wedged the last page between the handle and the rice paper scroll, rolled it up, rose, walked to the counter and gave it back to the librarian. I felt that my great-great-great-grandmother, Tsuiri Su-e, had written her diary for me alone.

I looked towards the doorway. Jun was already outside. I could clearly see his face. I ran towards him, as if crossing a field.

The Missing Vermeer

There are no portraits or self-portraits of Vermeer.

OUR LOVES, AS WE AGE, ARE ARBITRARY AND INEXPLICABLY TENDER, and this is particularly true for those who find themselves detached from the lives of the people around them or old before their time.

Kurosu Katsumi was just such a man. The right sentimental melody played by chance as background music in a shop or restaurant, a single leaf skitting sideways outside his window, the sight of a pretty young woman engrossed in a task, oblivious to anyone else in the picture ... or the thought of one painting that, try as he may, he could not sweep from his mind. These were the things that set a wave in motion inside him, flowing up through his throat, like acid, and out an eye.

'Oh dear,' he thought, when this wave overtook him, as it inevitably did at least once a day, 'I have been recreated in this world as a hopeless crybaby, at the tender age of fifty-six. If only my mother could see me now.'

No one could see him, no one, that is, who would recognise him. Leaving Tokyo, leaving home, leaving everyone who knew him was the only way to form a blank in the mind, to rid his eye of the insidious tear.

He whispered to himself: 'Every thought from now on will be disassociated with the man you were before. The old Kurosu Katsumi was left behind in Japan. Kurosu Katsumi, you are a new man, as yet without a new name. Kurosu Katsumi, you have no home, no wife, no children, no country, and certainly no longer any job. You are a traveller of the world, a blank slate of a man flung into the air, set free on a journey to wherever.'

These thoughts cheered him up no end, so much so that he was forced to cover the enormous smile on his lips with the back of his hand.

'Mustn't let anyone here think that I am out of the ordinary,' he thought, lifting his empty wine glass and tipping it on a ninety-degree angle, waiting for the last reluctant red drop to roll into his mouth.

He looked around, one eye taking in the entire café through the glass, distorting tables, walls and faces into a single spherical image, the jumble of voices reaching his ears warped into the monotone of an incomprehensible drone.

'I like this,' he thought. 'Music to my ears. It is as if both the sound and the light are reaching me from another time, a time I have no way of comprehending, a time I would prefer living in to this.'

He held the glass up to his eye like that, his very own glass chamber through which he could observe a world lit to his liking.

What had brought Kurosu Katsumi, ex-executive, dutiful husband and sometimes reasonable father to the Golden Lantern Café and Bar in Delft, Holland on this dull March day?

'I know what it is,' he thought, gradually lowering the glass and watching the image of the room and its people disperse into its separate clamourous parts. 'It's this little picture of intersecting lines at the bottom of the glass. This is what I came here to see.'

Holding the glass by its stem, he rotated it between his thumb and forefinger. The reflection of the leadlight window behind him circled the bottom of his glass.

'Ah, my own private kaleidoscope. I must be drunk, then. The reflection of the window, with its cut colours, should remain vertical at the bottom of my wine glass, despite the glass's rotation. Interesting, the facts one retains from one's high school science class. Without recalling that, I wouldn't know whether I have had a glass too many.'

He put down the wine glass methodically, so as to ease it onto the table without making a noise. The glass must have caught the light from the coloured paper lanterns hanging from the ceiling, for it was now streaked in red, gold and silver. A raucous laugh burst from his throat, and he covered his mouth again, staring around the room while trying to remain as inconspicuous as he could. He poured the last drops of wine from the carafe into his glass and took a sip of it, again surveying the room to make sure that no one was noticing that he was there.

Now the wine tasted bitter to him, as if the light from the leadlight window had somehow turned it. He put down the glass and lit a cigarette, inhaling deeply.

'I will glide from place to place without making a mark on anyone or anything,' he thought. 'I have severed myself from my roots. I've put Japan and family and home behind me. I am as free as a bird.'

He coughed several times, resting the cigarette in the groove in a large ceramic ashtray advertising Cinzano, and finished drinking the wine in his glass. Smoke filled the entire room now. It was as if everyone was now smoking in concert with him. He put the cigarette out and gestured to the young waitress. When he caught her eye, he pointed to the carafe and held up his forefinger, smiling. She nodded, swivelling about, and walked around the counter where the pony-tailed bartender was standing with his back to the customers.

The next thing Kurosu Katsumi knew he was beside a canal holding his head in his hands, a charming sight that no Dutch master, however sensitive to the sights of his town, would have imagined: 'Japanese with tousled black hair and head in hands on the edge of a Delft canal'. In his own eyes, when he finally dared open them, the canal itself was racing across the sky, upside down, streaking through a blanket of grey cloud, miraculously not spilling a drop of its contents, lighter than the air itself.

'More like Chagall than anything else. Oh, I mustn't be that drunk if I can make an observation like this.'

But no sooner had that thought occurred to him than a stream of reddish liquid, somewhat thicker than wine, spewed from his mouth straight down into the canal. His head was pounding, and, gripping his temples, his fingers a vice, he lay down along the cobbled embankment, staring sideways at the street.

The young waitress from the Golden Lantern, dressed in a white mini-skirt, navy tights and a light-blue pullover, passed him on her bicycle. He couldn't see her face clearly, but he recognised her by her shoulder-length blonde hair. The two wheels of the bicycle merged into four, then eight, then a line of revolving spokes with white, pink and blue edges.

'I'm going to be sick again,' he thought, digging his fingernails into his temples.

But just then she slowed down and turned her head back towards him, flashing a big smile.

'Oh my God,' he thought, 'that's all I needed. This beautiful young woman is trying to destroy Kurosu Katsumi forever!'

He put his head over the embankment, fully expecting an ochre stream to pour from his lips. But nothing came out, just a dry retching. He felt as if there was a rope connecting his stomach to his throat.

The canal itself listed, a black stripe painted in perspective, narrowing as it led into a corner of the canvas sky.

Two days later, in Amsterdam, while on his way from Central Station to Schiphol Airport, a woman with a multicoloured shawl covering her hair approached him on the train. She held an emaciated little boy on her hip. She thrust a note in front of his face. It read, in English …

I am from Afghanistan. Please help me. My husband was shot and killed.

The woman stared directly into his eyes. Even the little boy was staring right at him. He reached into his pocket and pulled out a twenty-euro note. The woman was not taking her eyes off of him, though the boy, who could not have been a day over three, took one look at the note and grabbed it from him.

When he arrived at the airport he immediately took the train back to Amsterdam, not bothering to cancel his flight to Dublin. The day before, he had thrown out half his clothes and his Samsonite suitcase in a skip that was sitting in the alley behind his Amsterdam hotel. He now carried everything he owned in a backpack.

He returned to Delft in the late afternoon. Why had he gone back? Was he searching for the waitress who turned her head to smile at him? Did he need to apologise to her, as any Japanese would wish to do, out of acute embarrassment? Was he hoping that she would turn a smile towards him once again?

He sat at the very same table by the leadlight window below the hanging Chinese lanterns, a full carafe of red wine, a wine glass and the Cinzano ashtray in front of him. He took out a cigarette, tossed it lightly in his palm and replaced it in its packet.

The waitress from the other day was nowhere to be seen. The person serving today was an exceedingly tall blonde waiter with five earrings in his left ear. Now it wasn't the wine or the glass or the light—and not even the thought of the angled canal—that bothered him. It was the Afghani woman and her little boy on the train. He could not get them out of his mind.

'I wasted that money,' he thought. 'That woman was making a fool out of me, and everyone on the train knew it. I could see in their eyes that they were telling me to ignore her. She was no doubt not an Afghani widow at all, but probably some European refugee who, for the price of the cheapest train ticket, knew she could cheat naive Japanese tourists of their money. I must not trust anyone.'

He pounded the table with his fist, causing a young couple sitting with both their hands joined across the table beside him to glance at him and chuckle.

'They're making fun of me, too. I am a Japanese wherever I go. I can escape myself, but there's no escaping the embarrassment inside me.'

'Bring me peanuts!' he shouted to the waiter who was rushing by. 'Peanuts now!'

The waiter nodded at him, picking up empty coffee cups and saucers from a nearby table.

'Now I am acting the boorish Japanese tourist,' he thought. 'Everybody will notice me. Everybody will hate me. Fine. It suits me. I deserve their scorn.'

Kurosu Katsumi laughed to himself, shaking his head. He didn't mind other people hating him. 'No one can despise me as much as I despise myself,' he thought.

The couple were now seated beside each other, kissing passionately. The young man, noticing him staring at them out of the corner of his eye, raised an eyebrow in indifference.

Kurosu Katsumi's mind, however, was elsewhere. He was recalling his wife admonishing him.

'You never had the ability to make decisions, except within the four walls of your office. I've never seen a person take so long to buy a single pair of socks. You stand in the department store in front of a display of socks as if your feet were nailed to the floor. Your eyes are glazed over, your jaw droops, your arms are as stiff as two poles. You'd think you were about to kill someone, not just pick out a simple pair of socks.'

Their two children were grown up, both working for trading companies, his son living in New York, his daughter in Nagoya, though she travelled back and forth to Hanoi once a month.

'They never have even a moment for their mother,' his wife complained. 'And neither do you have time for me, not really. Sometimes I don't know why we just go on living like this, Katsumi.'

It had started to rain heavily, and Kurosu Katsumi had still not poured his wine. The light coming through the leadlight window, a sheet of uniform grey, was not casting a shadow. He stared into the palms of his hands, then jerked his head up abruptly. He hadn't seen them leave, but the young couple were gone.

The chime over the front door of the Golden Lantern rang, and the waitress from the other day, wrapped in a wet black raincoat, walked in. She raised her elbows into the air and shook her body like a dog, sending drops of water against the door and floor. She took the raincoat off and hung it on the black iron coat rack beside the door. She was wearing the same white mini-skirt, navy tights and light-blue pullover as the day before.

'Hello again,' she said to him as she breezed by his table.

He quickly picked up the carafe, poured himself a full glass of wine. But again it tasted bitter, like the medicine of his childhood.

'Good man, Katsumi,' he said to himself. 'You can change red wine into medicine. You work miracles. This may be the medicine you need. Good man.'

He had walked out of his house in Tokyo without a word of warning to anyone. How could he explain this to his wife anyway? She would understand once he'd left. He thought, 'She was the one who said, "I don't know why we just go on living like this". That gave me my push. Whether the children would understand my actions or not didn't matter. I simply had to leave.'

'You took early retirement at fifty-five so that you would be able to study your art books and maybe even do some writing on art for the magazines,' his wife had said to him. 'But all you do is lie on your back at home as if your precious pictures were somehow hidden in the grain of the wood of the ceiling like a child's puzzle. You've even stopped looking up things on your computer. You've become totally useless to us all, including yourself.'

'Useless to us all, including myself...' he thought. 'An apt expression that describes me to a T.'

The waitress interrupted his train of thought.

'*Konnichiwa* (Hello),' she said.

'Wha...? You speak Japanese!'

'Well, just *sukoshi*, a little. I am a student of Japanese in Leiden, second year. I've never been there, to Japan, I mean. But my home's in Delft, so I come here to do this side job when I can.'

'*Arubaito.*'

'What?'

'It means side job in Japanese.'

'Doesn't sound like Japanese. You don't really look Japanese either.'

'I don't?'

He had never been so flattered in his entire life. There was nothing more wonderful you could say to Kurosu Katsumi than 'you don't look Japanese.'

'*Wine motto kureru?*' asked the waitress, pulling the hem of her pullover down over her waist.

'Are you asking me to give you some wine?'

'No. Oh, obviously I was mixing up the two words for "give". It's so difficult. One for when you give something to someone, and another for when someone else gives you something.'

'No, it's very good. I understand completely.'

He smiled at her, flicking his fourth finger nervously against the stem of his glass. For a moment, all he wanted to do for the rest of his life was teach this young Dutch woman correct Japanese.

'I must look ridiculous to her,' he thought, 'with my gritted teeth and lower lip stretched out in an artificial smile. How ugly I must look to her! I *do* look Japanese. I am even unable to smile without putting on a face that makes me appear disgusted with something, like Japanese men from the past in sepia photographs. Disgust for everything, especially disgust for self. That's me in a nutshell.'

'Well,' she said, tipping her head back and brushing the hair off her shoulders with the back of her hand, '*arigato gozaimasu*, thank you very much.'

'*Kochira koso* (No, I thank you). And I must apologise for my awful behaviour the other day.'

She shook her head, beaming, and walked towards the counter.

He stepped out of the Golden Lantern, passing houses made of half-size bricks with dates—1632, 1675—carved into stone above the doors. He would remain in Delft. He would not go back to Japan. He was useless in Japan, or so he thought.

THE NINETEENTH-CENTURY SCHOLAR THÉOPHILE THORÉ REFERS TO it only once ...

'After Vermeer died, the bankruptcy document mentioned a small painting, "vigourous and artful", of a man kneeling before his young model who is pregnant, wearing a yellow jacket with fur trim. The woman, as is uncharacteristic of this artist, has her back to us and the man is face on.'

This may have been the artist's own face.

The painting has not survived. Vermeer's face is invisible to us to this day.

'Who knows,' thought Kurosu Katsumi, 'I may discover it. I may very well be the man who will see Vermeer's face for the first time in over three hundred years!'

He continued to walk up and down every little street in Delft, with one thing on his mind. This one thing edged sentimental melodies, whirling leaves and even the smiles of a beautiful young woman out of the picture. The intense light of his mind now was focused on one thing only.

'I will look for the face of the artist as if it was my own. This will give me a reason for living, a use in life. The use is in the search. Good man, Kurosu Katsumi, good man!'

He continued to walk like that in a straight line, skirting a canal and beaming to himself all the while.

He now had something to do.